Working It Out

A Novel

Larry Smith

Best, Larry Smith

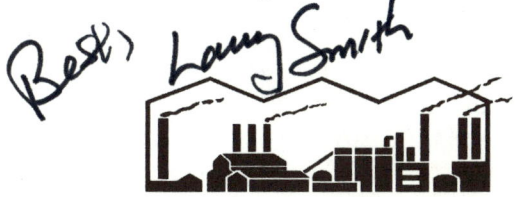

Ridgeway Press
Roseville, Michigan

© 1998
Larry Smith
ISBN 1-56439-071-3

Acknowledgments
Front Cover by Charles Cassady, Jr.
Author Photos by Kat Neyberg

The author wishes to thank the Ohio Arts Council for an Individual Artist Fellowship support grant for 1997-1998. The following portions of this novel first appeared in these publications:
"Housing" (under the title "Houses and Work")
in *New Waves* 1997
"Tracing It" and "Walking Inside"
in *The Heartlands Today: The Urban Midwest* 1997.

These poems are published with permission
"The Red Wheel Barrel" is by William Carlos Williams,
from *Collected Poems: 1909-1939*, Volume I. copyright 1938
by New Directions Publishing Corp.
and "In Memory of Kathleen" by Kenneth Patchen from
The Collected Poems of Kenneth Patchen copyright 1939, 1967
by New Directions Publishing Corp.
Carolyn Banks essay "Growing Up Polish in Pittsburgh"
appeared in *American Mix* edited by the author.
Portions of "The Owl's Bedtime Story" are from
Fly by Night by Randall Jarrell,
1969, Farrar, Strauss, & Giroux.

The author wishes to thank publisher M. L. Liebler,
Michael Waldecki, The Firelands Writing Center,
and my wife Ann and daughter Suzanne for
their care for and faith in this book.

This is a work of fiction; any resemblance between characters and living persons is purely coincidental. The place and times are real.

WORKING IT OUT

CHAPTERS

Tracing a Path   5
Walking Inside   9
Weighing the Words   13
Working Around It   17
Breathing It   20
Choosing It   24
Measuring the Work   27
Eating American Pie   33
Depending On It   40
Milking It   47
Reading Papers   49
Housing   53
Counting Our Losses   57
Getting the Word   60
Doing What Can Be Done   62
Molding the Shape of Things   68
Standing the Line   70
Watching Things Rise   76
Waking to It   79
Turning the Inside Out   81
Witnessing Three Wonders   84
Laying People Off   89
Learning By Going   92
Laboring   96
Delivering   100
About the Author   103

This book is dedicated to
Rosa

And to all the struggling couples who
have been or are working it out together.

In particular to:
Bill and Chris
Deb and Jean
John and Sue
Denny and Alice
Brian and Anna
Allen and Laura
Larry and Ann

TRACING A PATH

I am sitting in my beat Ford Fairlaine in downtown Lorain, Ohio, my incredibly shrinking city. I'm on Fifth Street at Oberlin Avenue which runs into the lake. The traffic light is red, but there is no traffic, only me waiting and watching at the crossroads. Outside my window I hear faint calls and wind it down—Canadian geese above the trees here in Lorain. I look up, and it's already too late. Over on Fifth Street though someone has come out of his place, one of those 1930's row houses, a dark brick, two-story company house. I wonder who owns them now that the steel mill has been sold again and again, each new company owner draining the blood from this town. This guy I'm watching just stands there on his little porch taking a big breath of the cool October air. Now he is brushing back his dark hair with the fingers of both hands. His work shirt flaps open in the breeze showing a white streak of a T-shirt which he pounds once with his fist and turns. I watch people like birds; why should I wait for eagles?

My light has changed and I cross, go right past his stoop, catch him checking me over and tilt my head up quick and smile. He stares for a moment then slowly tips his head back. We recognize each other: strangers in a city we share.

At the corner of Cornell I look left to the old Antler Hotel complex and the public sculpture in the park. It's a tent-like affair all blown and worn. It always reminds me of the Lorain shipyards now closed forever after the last stand-off between company and labor. All those jobs and all those huge ore ships now gone, turning our lift bridge into a gesture to the absurd. I hear myself think-talk and wonder just when I started thinking this way. Was it before or after I started taking classes out at the community college—I mean, philosophy, political science, literature. Maybe the thoughts were always there without the words. I hope I'm not ingesting that *college way* of thinking, any more than I wanted to inherit that *mill thought and talk*.

Christ, I'm thirty and a survivor...of what...the loss of my parents and sister, the ravishes of our local drug scene, the wounds of mill closings and strike violence. Hey, if we're still here, we're survivors, right? More than fighting or fleeing, it's a question of being a survivor or a victim. The light is green, and so I turn.

Last night in our little apartment I joked with Maria about my graduation. "Well, in a few weeks I'll complete my learning. I'll know everything. You can ask me anything — absolutely anything. You can begin any time, really."

Maria looked up from the couch and with a look as pregnant as she, said, "Don't worry, honey. I'm sure life has plenty more to teach you." You can't get ahead of Maria, no how.

At Reid Avenue I pass Rudy's Deli where I used to work — closed now and dead looking like an abandoned refrigerator, or a supermarket cart in an alley. I can't help wondering where all those customers get their breakfast now. I mean, it used to get so loud and lively in there, people nursing coffee or a cigarette, talking that morning talk...*What about the new mayor? What have they done to our Browns? Who's the new waitress with the ribbon in her hair?*...God, I miss them all. I do. And though I swore never to pick up, much less wash, another heavy diner dish, I'd do it all day long if I could turn those Deli lights back on.

Today I am headed elsewhere, for a job interview — teaching, can you believe it? English, no less! This is my third, second-interview. What you do is you go out to their school and they show you around the building and treat you to a cafeteria lunch. My first one was in Vermillion Schools, a pretty town along the lake — Harbor City they call it — old store fronts taking you back to a New England town. I don't think I'll get that job though. The assistant principal actually called my adviser and complained that my handshake was too weak. Yeah, like his office coffee.

The second, second interview was at Amherst Schools, south of Lorain — a junior high, though I was hoping for high school. The woman principal, Mrs. Slater, said I handled myself well in the teaching demonstration with seventh graders. I don't know, maybe I did, but the kids were so loud and talky, I thought I missed them. The boys were smirking mostly, and several of the girls kept giving me the eye. What I did with them was a session on writing details — specific and concrete, those factual and sensory words. At the end of it I had them write a haiku poem. They got into that. I think the best one was from a small boy in the back row:

> My father's hands
> are fine and nervous
> on the lug wrench.

I don't care that they couldn't count syllables. The feeling and thought came together there. He let an image tell its story....Anyway, I may get an offer from them, I don't know.

Today I'm talking with the folks at Lorain's St. Mary's Catholic School—another elementary and junior high, but for about two-thirds the pay. When I first met the principal at the college interview, a street-clothes nun named Sister Agnes, she right away announced, "We're a strong science school." I didn't know what to say since that isn't really my area. "We maintain strict discipline," she added, but I still didn't speak. Then she eyed my bad leg and asked if I could coach. I felt my refusal had sunk my chances, but when I told her that I grew up in West Lorain and that I lived now a couple blocks away, she stared back into my eyes. Who knows what she was reading, but she did smile and whisper, "You must come see our schools." She made a check mark beside my name and closed her book. I felt as though I had made the cut, though I still wasn't on the team.

I pass the Lorain Public Library on Sixth Street—a long, bright windowed building, always busy. And always there is a guy or woman in a security uniform patrolling the front door...people stealing books I suppose. Seems people in Lorain don't trust each other or themselves. I pull onto Eighth Street at the side of St. Mary's School...dark brick buildings gathered beside a stone church on the corner. Layers of classrooms with bright windows are spread beside and above me. On the first floor autumn leaves and pumpkin faces look out at me, all of them cut neat and from the same pattern. Upstairs I can see girls and boys passing the windows in blue sweaters and white shirts. It is exactly seven, twenty-five, as I open the car door and walk toward my fate.

WALKING INSIDE

Yes, the walls are bare and the floors are clean, as you'd expect. And yes, a wooden crucifix hangs at the front of every room along with an American flag. This much I expected. But as I walk down the hallway to "Report to the Principal's Office," I can smell the quiet. It's like walking through the woods at first when the animals go into hiding; no, there isn't even that much sound. It's more like the stillness of walking into an empty church. It's an atmosphere that surrounds me, but I don't know how to read it or what it really means. I look out at the noisy city streets, and inside is this stillness.

I come to the end of the hallway up against a voice: "Good morning students and staff," There's a pause in which I can hear from each classroom the echo of voices answering back, "Good morning, Sister." Then, "Children, let us remember this morning that each life is a gift." There is another pause in which I recognize Sister Agnes' voice amplified. "And remember that each of us leaves our special mark. Do your best—meet the test. Now, say it with me. You know it, I'm sure, 'Good, better, best; never let it rest, until your good is better, and your better best.'" A choral echo rises from each room. "Now, Marie Lepanski from Mrs. Thompson's fifth grade class will lead us in prayer."

I am standing there with my head bowed asking myself how much I believe in this good—better—best philosophy when a clear sweet voice announces. "In the name of the Father, the Son, and the Holy Ghost." I start to cross myself, look around, and let my hand drop. Little Marie takes us through our daily blessings and closes with, "We ask for your guidance and your special light as we do the work we must. Thank thee oh Lord for thy precious gifts Thou has given to us. In thy holy name, A-men."

I am standing at the white porcelain fountain and shaking in my new tight shoes. If this simple act of orchestrated devotion can so rattle me, what would teaching here be like? I haven't been to a Mass since our wedding, or confessed to a priest for way too many years. Heck, I didn't even go to Catholic schools. We were "publics" in a parochial neighborhood. Each year Mom and Pop would have this one out. "Listen, Woman," Dad would say like a cop, "We can't afford it—ain't got the money. Can't pay the Franciscans three tuitions to go to no Catholic school." And each year Mom would come back with, "But, Hank, I told you already, every year the church sponsors so many children of need." She had said that fatal word, "need." "I'll tell you what we need. We don't need no charity—we got our public schools!" And though each year my brother Ted would fall further behind in reading and math, till he dropped out of Admiral King at 16, Dad still held to his position. If she pressed him further, he would claim his own sacred right, that of separating church and state. It was his private religion then...that and a bottle of Seagrams Seven. On Sundays at our house, Mom would leave the spaghetti sauce on to simmer and rush off to Mass with us kids. When we were in junior high, Ted and I would loaf at home with Dad who'd be smoking his way through the newspaper. We'd all drink coffee and make toast till Mom and JoAnn got home. Mom would set the church bulletin on the kitchen table, say, "You heathens missed a wonderful homily by Father Daley. Didn't they, JoAnn?" who would always nod real big. And me, all grubby and yawning still, I'd feel like the scum of the earth. "The Good Lord loves us all," Dad said once, and walked out the back door and fell right off the porch.

  That same sinner's feeling is creeping up my spine now, along my neck, toward my head as the principal's door flies open and a small-faced woman in a tan suit comes out. Tears are streaming down her face. She doesn't look up at me, just ducks her way into the little girls' room. Suddenly I want to go home, sit at the kitchen table, and smoke cigarettes all morning, but I know Maria would be there asking me, "Well, how did the interview go?" She would look down at her belly and we'd both want to build some dreams on the promise of a job.

I walk in.

"Ah, Mr. Marco Lorenz, I presume." It is Sister Agnes, glancing at the clock, saying, "Five minutes late—that means a detention." It takes me a moment to recognize that the Sister has a sense of humor.

"Sister Agnes," I say and give the penitent nod.

"This way," she says and brushes past me and through the glass threshold of her office. There are windowed partitions and no doors—on the wall are neat rows of hard covered books, most of them texts. The back window holds a small pot of purpled chrysanthemums. It is all as clean and efficient as her tan suit.

"Sister Agnes, forgive me, but outside just now there was a woman who seemed pretty upset."

A quick glance, "That is Sister Anne, and not really your concern."

I can see this job draining down the ochre walls onto the floor, and I'll admit I begin to feel a little light headed and hearted. Then I think of Maria and the future Baba greeting me all open eyed and tender.

"I'm sorry. You're right. I'm here for the interview."

"Obviously," she says in almost a smile and sits down in her office chair.

Beside her is a nice computer screen, and I need to change the subject, so I ask, "Is that one of the new Dell Pentiums?"

"Yes, it is. 32 Meg of Ram. Are you, by any chance, computer literate, Mr. Lorenz?"

"Yes, I am...to an extent. I'm no technician, but I can navigate the Web, download a CD Ram, install soft and hardware. Mostly I use the word processing..." (Always hard to know how much to disclose) "...for my writing. I'm a writer."

She rocks back in her swivel desk chair, taps her pencil on her desk pad, "And what type of writing would that be...articles and essays?"

"No. Mostly I write fiction...and poetry. But I can handle a press release or a grant proposal. I've done it at the college relations office." I can't believe how I'm pitching myself.

Again she almost smiles, taking notes all the while, then asks, "May I call you Marco?" Of course, I nod yes. "Well, before we take the tour of the plant and meet people, I'll ask you what I ask all of our candidates. Can you tell me, please, why it is you want to teach?"

I pause for only a moment, swallow the school air, and say what's there, "Because, Sister Agnes. Life *is* a precious gift, as you say." Then tasting cotton in my throat, I look her straight in the eyes, "And each of us, Sister, does have a talent, or gift, that only works when we give it away. I think mine is teaching."

WEIGHING THE WORDS

Walking down the hallway, I am thinking I have nailed this teaching job—One out of three is good enough for me. I decide to go upstairs where the junior high rooms are. Suddenly I hear the school bell and doors come flying open. I am caught in a stream of rushing sixth and seventh and eighth graders; the precious silence of St. Mary's has been broken. These students are more wide and wild eyed. No one shouts but everyone seems to be talking. I wonder who is left to listen, but realize everyone is listening as well, like birds. Words have power here even if they are cast about, and believe me everyone is counting.

One girl bumps into me, her hair the color of melting pennies. She looks at my cane and almost begins to cry. "Oh, dear God, I am sorry, please forgive me."

"It's nothing," I say, "It's my own stupid fault for not watching." I realize right away I have gone too far with that "stupid," for she takes it up.

"Oh, yes, it was really so stupid of me." She means it, I can tell in her eyes, and I want to release her from any obligation.

"You are forgiven, my child," I say, laying on the priestly tone.

"Thank you," she says and nods, rushing off to join her crowd, and just in time to make it into a classroom. I see Sister Anne at the doorway, and her eyes are still as red and puffy as buns. It is afterall her job for which I am interviewing. In a week Sister Anne will not only be gone, but she will not be Sister any longer. It's none of my business really, but I've already learned of her romance with lay teacher, Mr. Weatherspoon. Romance has bloomed among the rocks here, and is promptly being stamped out. Going down the stairs, I ask myself: Is this my problem? I decide no, it is not.

I have to pick up some things before driving home to Maria, so I turn the radio to the NPR station, 91.3. What do you know, they are talking about war. Ever since Dr. Howard's Poli-Sci course, I have been tuning into the news from NPR. At home we've started listening to "All Things Considered" and "Fresh Air." I even subscribed to the *Christian Science Monitor* for two months, but had to quit. I just couldn't keep up. Don't get me wrong, I still think they are a necessary alternative to our standard media news, but knowing it all becomes overwhelming. Right now, for example, if you listen to just the tone of the radio voices you can hear an insistence that rivals the station's static for irritation. Why does everything have to be so dire and diligent if you're informed? And the language: "romantic militancy," "flagrant violation of human rights," "the price of diligence"...My gosh, "bear any burden, pay any price..." It's all really heroic to care about so much, and when you're of a mind for it, it's great, but sometimes, admit it, it does grate on the nerves. Right now for example I am feeling the pain of hearing about murdered Bosnian children at the same time I feel the sweet relief of having found a new job. The conflict in my head is causing me pain, and so, forgive me, I have to switch off.

  As I pull alongside of the house we are renting on Seneca Avenue near South Lorain, I notice Margaret's car parked along the street. Margaret is Maria's best friend, and has been since they grew up not far from here in the projects. Something seems funny though; maybe it's the angle of the tires next to the curb. I take my paper and the mailers picked up from Office Max and I go into the house. We live upstairs, something Maria sings about every time we go in or out. "My God, these steps. How many? How few to go? Why are there any?"
  Our place is so near the mill you can smell its sooty ripeness whenever you're outside. When we kids used to complain about the smell, Dad would shush us with, "That's the smell of work, kids, the work that feeds you. Get used to it." Well, that smell has grown pretty faint in this town. I think we invented downsizing here in Lorain. This town is performing a real vanishing act as we speak.

And so, I come into a cozy scene after all. Maria and Margaret—sitting before the television drinking coffee, eating Girl Scout Thin Mints and raging over the soaps.

"Hey, Margaret, who parked your car for you, your cat? Or were you driving blind?" I don't know why I am always a wiseass around Margaret, maybe it's because we both love Maria so much.

"Bravo, Marco. You've just insulted your pregnant wife."

I face Maria, "What? Why were you driving Margaret's car?"

Maria is calm, "Come on in here, Marco, there's nothing to get upset about. Sit down and I'll get you a nice cup of coffee." We kiss hello as she passes. "I just needed a lift to the grocery store with Margaret, and she asked me to drive home."

I cast a glance at Margaret, who casts it up to the ceiling. I make the Italian gesture for Why?—shoulders and palms raised slightly. I get back a shrug.

"Oh, yeah, and we stopped for a few minutes at the hospital."

"What!"

"Now, take it easy, Honey. Didn't I say everything was okay? Do you want a roll with your coffee. We stopped at Dunkin' Donuts."

I go over to Maria, take both her hands in mine. They are still trembling. "Are you and the baby okay?"

She is still trying to smile it away, yet her eyes are clearly sad. "Yes. I'm okay, Marco. It was just a little bleeding, and it stopped before we got there. They looked me over and sent me home. They told me to stay off my feet for a while. I have an appointment with Dr. Lorri tomorrow, can you take me?"

"Yes, are you sure, though? You feel okay?" I take the cup from her hands. It has my cream and sugar already mixed inside. I lead Maria to the couch.

"It's okay, Marco. I'm okay. The baby's okay. I just got a little scared. Oh, how did your interview go this morning?"

I had forgotten to call her. Now I am having trouble remembering for what. "Oh, yes, my God, I forgot! Maria, I think I got it, the job at St. Mary's teaching seventh and eighth grade English."

They both clap, and now I am shaking a little. "What exactly did they say?" It is Margaret who asks now.

"The principal, Sister Agnes, she said there was one more person to interview, but that things looked good. My grades and recommendations were strong, and she liked my knowing about computers and public relations."

"Public relations?" It is Margaret again.

"Okay, I told them that I was a writer and that I knew how to write press releases. It's not a lie you know."

"Yeah, sure, and I'm the Queen of Sheba. Come on!"

"Margaret, please, don't ruin this." It is Maria come to my rescue. "You know how it is, you say things in a job interview. No one expects it all to be true. Right?"

I am wishing Margaret would just migrate like the Canadian geese. Canada might be a good destination. Maybe she'd make it across the lake, maybe not. Anyway, it is almost time for her to go to work. She's a cashier at Sam's Wholesale Club down around the Midway Mall and a waitress at El Patio Restaurant in South Lorain.

Maria just keeps looking at me sweet and softly, eyeing me to wait; it will be alright. Then Margaret jumps up, says, "Oh, my God, I'm late," and is gone. When Maria comes over to me she hugs me so that there is for a moment the three of us in one embrace, our little trinity — Maria and baby and me.

WORKING AROUND IT

Soon I am to graduate from this college with a degree—Bachelor's of Arts and Sciences. Only for a year Maria and I have been married, so I'm not a bachelor. I'm also no scientist, and the only art I really know is my writing. To tell you the truth, it feels like trying on another man's suit.

I am sitting here at the Health Department's Clinic thinking about all this while Maria is inside having a prenatal exam from Dr. Lorie Esposito, an obstetrician. While I've been carrying around a Grade Point Average, she has been carrying our little Maria or Marco junior. There's no way to compare the two—it would be like weighing wind and water.

I'm writing this down bit by bit in this journal, so I'm keeping it in present tense. You get the feeling of it happening. Maybe, one day it could turn itself into a novel.

Oh, the dark eyed girl in the corner who came in with her mother has just run into the little bathroom—a place Maria seems drawn to like a cat to tuna. Even with her big belly, Maria can move like a cat-woman. Ah, that huge curve of her body has become the source of our pleasure and pain. I love stroking it, rubbing the soft globe of it with baby oil. The doctor said my rubbing might help with the stretch marks, but I think she just wanted to give me something to do—a science project. Maria loves it though—it's one time she never complains—"Oh, Marco, do it some more, please. Back here around the sides more." Then she smiles deep and sighs like a kitten, "I love your hands," and who can resist?

To tell the truth, I have to watch it. You know, getting a-roused. I'm torn now, I tell you, between the mother and the child. Since we did that Sonogram thing where you can hear and see the baby inside the womb, I can't do it without feeling like an alien invading his soft world with my hard thrusting penis. It's strange, you have to admit.

Oh, I want her plenty, but I also want her safe. It's all driving me quietly nuts inside.

It won't go away. I know that now. Like, when we went down to her mother's place for dinner last Sunday — oh, boy! Esther greets us at the door, makes Maria take off her coat and show her huge belly — "Oh, muchacha, tanto grande!" When she smiles back at me, I just grin. Then Esther turns and she asks it, "Well, Marco, how do you like it?"

"Like what?" I ask dumbly and wait.

"How do you like *riding the hump* — huh?" Well, there is a full five seconds of silence; then everyone roars with laughter and begins pointing my way. Even Esther blushes with me as she looks to Maria, "I'm sorry," she says, "that's what my father asked your father each time I was pregnant." She is hugging Maria's soft dome and crying for joy as I pass, slipping through the doorway and into the quiet kitchen.

Maria's step-dad Luis is there. He is always in this kitchen drinking slowly at his table from short, thin glasses.

"Marco," he says rising, "Come join me," and he holds out a glass of honey colored liquid. It is warm to the palm. He squeezes the muscle of my arm with his powerful hand. Years of truck farming in the Ohio fields have turned his arms and hands to stone.

"Sip it, my son. Drink slowly as the sun goes down."

"What is this, Luis?" I have to ask, for one sip has already taken me somewhere far out on the horizon where the sun is just above the trees.

Luis tilts his head slowly. "It's a drink from my native land: a mixture of tea and honey..."

"And...what else?" I nod, grinning.

He too nods, "Some Tequilla... and your Southern Comfort."

I sip again and it rolls gently over my tongue melting its way down my throat. It holds one quiet, turns the women's voices to music. I sit and I sip.

"*Golondrina*, it's called. *Golon-drina* — it's Mexican for the swallows," and he turns his hands into flapping birds. "Someday I teach it to you. Okay?"

"Sure...mucho, Luis. Mucho." And for the first time in a month I am rested. I can feel my heart rate slow to the movement of the sun into the trees. My breath follows the snow geese over the back field. I am inside this dream liquid as Luis pours us another.

"Marco, I'm going to tell you the story that goes with this drink. You've heard of how the swallows, the birds, they go back to San Juan Capistrano, si'?"

"Si'" I'm thinking Spanish now.

"Well, what you do not know is how my people celebrate this. On that day they walk over the border from Mexico and they go to sit all day in the warm sun, sipping glass after glass of *Golondrina*. They drink and they watch the birds come in, till the sun it goes down. Then they walk back across the border to their homes."

Luis reads my big smile as part of the landscape now, and it really is. I am already there with him in his place, feeling the warm descent of the sun.

"Soon," he says, softly reaching over to pat my hand. "Soon enough, you will have your Maria back again...and a child too to hold your dreams. Till then," and he raises his glass slowly in the last trace of sun, "we drink life together." And we do.

Thinking this now, as I sit in this clinic waiting for Maria, I cup my hands at my lap, lean back and close my eyes, and I feel the full sun floating into my cup.

BREATHING IT

Maria waits till I come around to open the door on her side. This old Fairlane is a two door with those big heavy doors that squeak open and shut like a barn door. It's the first car that we bought together as husband and wife, yet Maria insisted that I put it in my name. "I won't be listed as the owner of this—jalopy," she said. "This car is yours, Marco, to drive till it dies. I'll wait till we get a little money in the bank and can afford a Mustang. Then, *caramba*! I'll own that one—my little red Mustang."

Tonight though, Maria is tired. I can see it in her dark eyes and the slow way she moves around. It's her eighth month, so I guess that's expected. What do I know—I've never had a child before.

The doctor said everything was okay with the baby. But she wants Maria to come back in next week. It won't be easy, especially if I get that job at St. Mary's. And, as much as Maria loves Dr. Esposito, she has this *thing* about going to doctors...like it's asking for trouble. For Maria, you increase your odds for illness the closer you live to a hospital. "A lot of people believe that," she says and turns her head away.

"Marco," she says as I begin to back the car out. "I need one of your hugs."

We kiss and I notice how warm her face is in my hands. Her hair smells sweet like that honeysuckle shower gel she loves to use. She's a beautiful sight all soaped up, belly and all, like a Cupey doll dipped in whipped cream. I sigh, then feel her hands in my hair. Right here in the health department parking lot she is biting my ear. I am touching the silk of her dress and feeling her almost naked beside me. I bite her ear back, and we both laugh. It is all candy and music for a sweet minute. Then we sit back and I reverse the Fairlane, then head it out of the drive. How is it passion creeps up when sex is impossible? A couple in bright jogging suits is walking quickly by, and I think to say, "Someday, that will be us."

"Can you imagine this body draped in nylon stripes?" Maria is happy again, relieved I think that everything is okay for a while. I trust this woman with my life, but I know her too. She can move through dark to sunny skies faster than anyone alive.

I'll tell you a story of this. Last summer, we took a drive to Mill Hollow Park, with its huge cliffs above the Vermillion River. It's a nice drive past trees and fields. Maria had been quiet all day, and when we stood by the stream looking up at the sky above the cliffs, she began to cry softly. We sat down on a huge limestone rock and held each other. I was crying too and neither of us knew why. I could never do this without Maria. When we stopped, I lay out on the rock, staring down at my image in the stream. The sun was directly overhead. Finally I looked into the water and asked, "Is this reflection me?"

Childlike she answered, "It's your image. It's not you." We could hear a breeze through the locust trees.

"But how does this water hold my image?" I wouldn't let up.

She spoke softly, "It holds you, Marco, with the skin of a mirror."

I thought about that then asked, "And where do we touch? This stream and me—where do we touch?"

I had her there, I thought, till she leaned over my shoulder to the water, said "Look," and splashed the stream into my face. We laughed about that again and again on the way to the ice cream place. Darkness and light, the light in the darkness, Maria knows them both.

See, Maria is so alive to things, so able to take them into herself, and yet move on to what's to be done. Take last Sunday, Esther calls and says Maria's brother Jose has been arrested again. "Mom. What for?" her voice pleads. "Grand theft—Jesus, Mary, and Joseph! What do you mean his company is charging him? Didn't they know he was borrowing their truck to help Lisa move? Oh, my God! They've got him in the Lorain County Jail." Maria screams and cries, hangs up, then throws herself on the couch. And then...and then her face looks hot so I go back into the bathroom to get a damp cloth to help cool her down. I let it warm a little then wring out the excess water, just a few seconds. When I return, it's to an empty room. Maria is up cleaning the kitchen counter, putting the afternoon dishes into the sink and wiping the counter. "If you feel like it," she says softly, "you could begin grinding down some cheese for the spaghetti sauce. Okay? It's almost ready." And there's nothing psychotic about all this, 'cause by the time the noodles are cooked, she has planned out how to get the bail money together, and I know that evening we'll be driving around town to collect from each of the family. She takes it all in and gives it all back, like a deep cleansing breath. She's a star of the natural childbirth class.

Heading down Lorain Boulevard now, I look out at all the cars parked along Oakwood Park, and Maria puts her hand on my arm. Her touch is so light, at first I don't notice. "Don't ever leave me," she says. "Don't ever leave me. Okay?" We just keep driving into the approaching dusk.

"I won't ever," I say. "You are safe with me." It feels almost spooky to say it right there like that, but I want her to know. Besides saving me from my life, she has become one with it. We both know this like our breath.

"I love you," I say driving ahead, and in the car comes its echo.

We are at the corner of 30th when I remember my promise to stop at El Patio for dinner. I know she has been counting on this all day. We slow around the corner and pull up to the railing in the parking lot. I shut off the engine and we get out.

Inside El Patio, we are greeted by Carmine who seats us at our table along the north wall near the seaside mural. It's nice, even though I know the millyards of Lorain Steel are only two blocks away. We each order the chicken burritos with beans and rice.

Out of the kitchen comes Margaret wearing the bright chef's apron that Maria bought her. She kisses Maria and asks, "Is everything alright...with the baby, I mean? Are you okay?" Maria nods three times. "I knew it," says Margaret. "Life bites you on the teat for nothing and then lets you go. You know it's true. Huh, Marco, huh?" and she reaches over, pinches my chest and twists. I push her away.

"Hey, Carmine, you better control your waitresses!" I shout, but she just sits down. And soon we are all drinking water and dipping chips into the salsa — me in the mild, Margaret in the hot, Maria in both. Then Carmine enters and sits two hot plates before us. The steam rises into Maria's smiling face. Margaret sneaks a bite of Maria's burrito, always feeding off of her.

"Go," I say, and she disappears into the kitchen. And then, Maria and I, we sit and eat it all, with our knife and our fork.

CHOOSING IT

On the drive back from the restaurant we keep saying names out loud in the car: Robert, Michael, Ronald, Paul—those are mine; Marianne, Esther, Esperanza, Carmela—Maria's, of course. When we get home it is there, a message on a machine. The little green light is flashing. Maria pushes the button and Sister Agnes speaks:

"Mr. Marco Lorenz, Please. This is Sister Agnes from St. Mary's Catholic School in Lorain. I call to inform you that our school board has met and decided to offer you the eighth grade teaching position for the remainder of the school year." There is a pause as she thinks or leaves time for me to absorb the news. "Call me tomorrow, Mr. Lorenz. If you are interested, we can meet to work out the details. If not, we can offer it to someone else who is."

Maria reads my face, but the print isn't clear. I had this sense that the call would come, yet suddenly I don't know if this is right for us. Am I being handed a balloon or an anchor? Those nuns—will I be able to ride on their wings or will I be cast off and put into chains? I pull a chair back around and sit down at the kitchen table. Maria draws us both a glass of water.

"Here, drink something," and she starts rubbing my shoulders slow and tender. "It could be a good thing, Marco, but I don't know. It's up to you."

"I know that," I say, but I also know we are all tied into it—Maria, baby, and me. I hear myself speak, "I don't know, Maria. It feels like...I don't know...like I'm stepping into wet cement. It could get me across or it could pull me in deep forever." She looks deep into my eyes. There is only the sound of our breathing.

Then I say, "I don't know what's bothering me, Maria. This should be a good thing. I know it. It's what we both have been working for. I'm just scared, afraid that I'll be...you know..."

"What?" coaxes Maria.

"Changed...forever changed!" I blurt out. "That I'll be someone not me." I have to get up and walk around. "Maybe you can explain it to me?" I plead with her eyes. She says nothing, just waits for me to walk it off. I am pacing like a dog needing out.

When I finally sit down again she says, "It's up to you, Marco. It's really your choice; you've earned it. But know please, my love, that you do have a choice. It's real. We can live with whatever you decide." She reaches her hand to mine, says, "I understand really. Remember when I did the pregnancy test and we first knew?"

"Of course, it was here at this table that you told me."

"Well...?"

"Yeah," I was starting to get it.

"Can you see what a big choice that was for me? And I felt like you, Marco, that things would be changed forever. Understand?" I nod and sit down on the chair across from her. "Listen, I told you about the time when I had an abortion. Remember? Well, even though I was only fourteen and the guy was a jerk who ran off. Even then, it was a hard decision for me, because my head and my heart were fighting." She is speaking a truth so deep from herself, trusting it will make things clearer for me.

"See, Marco, I knew I couldn't care for that child, but my heart, my heart, pulled me to love it just the same. I was caught, but I still had a choice—it was still there for me to make. Some people like my grandmother, they had no choice. Others like my mother and Aunt Esperanza, they fought for choice. I knew I had to be worthy of that, even as I had to take on the pain of the loss of that child. But this child, our child, Marco, even if you spit on me and walked out that door forever, I would have it—because I love it and you and I can care for it now. It's a choice I've earned, see. And your working so hard for four years at the college, that has earned this choice for you."

She is staring right into my soul, and slowly like a movie zooming back I am able to see it. This isn't my whole life. I could say yes or no tomorrow and be the same man. It's not about right and wrong, it's about making a decision. Maria reaches to hug me, and I move across, hold her head next to mine.

"I don't need to sleep on it, cause I probably won't sleep anyway. We'll take it and do it for all it's worth, Maria. In a couple of days, I'll be Mr. Lorenz, St. Mary's new lay instructor, English eighth grade."

Maria smiles at that like she does, with her clear dark eyes, and we both rise to dress for bed.

She has been sleeping now for two hours, while I'm wide awake, writing this and teaching fragments and run-ons in the classroom of my head.

MEASURING THE WORK

After my talk with Sister Agnes I decide to drive over to my brother Ted's place on Homewood Drive in South Lorain. He's working the afternoon shift today, and it's already one o'clock, so he'll be home. I gave Maria the good news over the phone. The job was about what we expected—teach out the year at a fair salary with full benefits, and then see what happens for next year.

This is Wednesday, so I had already dropped Maria off at Esther's place before I went to St. Mary's. This is the day they do each other's hair—Maria and her mom—two women drinking coffee and talking about 'things.' Many times I have sat at that formica table and eaten big ham and tomato sandwiches with them, mostly listening to their talking. Luis is usually gone—down at the E-Lite Tavern in Amherst where he sits at the bar talking or playing cards with his old buddies. I've been there with him. When I was going to Lorain Community College this was a regular Wednesday scene. Now I'll have to hear all about it from Maria.

I want to tell Ted about this job because he's the one who kept pushing me towards college. Every semester he bought my books and his wife Marge gave me rides whenever our car would die. She'd pick me up and drop me off—"You're just one of my kids," she'd joke, and I admit, I liked having someone care for me like Mom.

As I pull up, I see Ted out in the driveway. The hood on his Ford Ranger is up, and the orange cord of his utility light is snaking its way across the driveway and under the engine.

"Hey!" I yell, walking up the drive.

"Hey, yourself!" comes from under the engine block. "Who that?" he calls.

"Who that say that who that?" I return.

"Who that who say that who that?" It's an old game of ours that we learned from Dad.

Bending over the engine, I see part of Ted's face. He has on brown winter coveralls, and his Cleveland Indians cap is tipped off his head and lying upside down in the driveway. He's losing more hair.

"Marco! What the heck are you doing here? And wearing a suit—Hell, man, did someone die?"

"Hey, Brother Ted, why don't you pull this heap into the garage?"

"Why should I?" he throws back. "For the neighbor's sake? Look around you." He is right; almost all the driveways have cars parked in them, several are up on blocks. "Besides," he spurts, "Where would I put it?"

I look into the garage—full of bikes and boxes, garbage cans, stored lawn furniture, an old broken clothes dryer and a rack of hanging coats. "Guess you're right. But come out of there a minute will you? I got something to tell you."

He slides out on the creeper, the metal wheels grinding away on the concrete.

Standing up, eyeing me now, he shakes his head, "Well, I can see you didn't come to help."

"I didn't know. What you working on anyway?"

"Radiator's started to leak, so I'm replacing it. There's the old one in the garage." And I read the wet rusted guts of it—a worn beehive of metal that reminds me most of the rows of empty buildings at USS/KOBE Steel, where Dad and Ted used to work.

"Well, what's the news?" he asks.

"Ted, by God, I've got a job."

"Yeah?" he looks up and into my eyes.

"Teaching school."

"No shit. Where at?"

"For now at St. Mary's—eighth grade English."

His grin broadens into a smile. "I'd hug you, but..." and we look down at his grease grey clothes. I step across the grass to embrace his square body. His strong arms surround me. It's a moment in the front yard, and we look around to see Marge with her camera snapping us.

"Maria called this morning," she laughs. "I got it out of her, but she said you wanted to tell Ted."

We are three happy people out in the yard. A car drives by and honks. Ted yells, "It's my brother—the teacher! He got himself a job." The driver smiles, then toots again. Ted turns to Marge, "Hey, Hon, we got any of that sheet cake of yours? Let's have some with coffee. Go ahead in, Marco, I'll shut down out here. Hell, I'll just finish it tomorrow."

Their house is always full of warmth and clutter. Marge is a wonderful cook, and her kitchen always looks 'used' and in the middle of something. Lunch plates are stacked on the counter along side of the microwave; bags of bread and bagels are bunched around the Mr. Coffee. On the stove is a pot of simmering beef stew.

"We're real proud of you," she says, handing me a heavy mug of coffee. "Come on in here. We'll sit at the table."

"I feel kind of funny about all this," I admit. "I haven't done anything yet but get hired."

"Hey, around this town, that's pretty major," she says, and we both laugh at the truth of it. "It's been a hard earned accomplishment, Marco. We all know that," and she pats my arm. I am moved into another hug, and I feel her soft heavy body trembling.

"Thanks, forever, Marge, to you and Ted. How would I have done it without you?"

Ted has entered through the garage. He has removed the winter coveralls and stands in jeans and that Browns T-shirt he refuses to put away. He is as tall as I am short, as broad as I am thin. People usually gasp, "You two are brothers!" Then they think about us and our ways, and they smile, "Yeah, now I can see it. You do resemble each other."

We are close, but not one. Our differences are small but loud. I will never forget that terrible scene we had right here at this table. It was two years ago during my sophomore year at LCCC. I had stopped over after class one morning to see if Ted wanted to go drive some golf balls.

"Golf—Where do you get this shit? What are you doing, Marco, becoming *middle class*?"

Wow, I thought. Where is this coming from?

"Forget it," I said, looking down at his left hand bleeding from the knuckles. "Hey, you better take care of that."

He held up his hand, "This here hand is the hand that just broke the nose of Frank McGee."

"What...?"

"I got into a damn fight with that Putz outside the UAW hall just now. We're looking at another strike, you know. Well, after the meeting, in the parking lot he wanted to get a bunch of us to go over to the company parking lot and bust up some windows in the company vans. I said no, it would cost us more than wages to start breaking property and laws. He called me a wimp. I took it. Only when I called him a terrorist, he took a swing at me, which I blocked. When he came at me with his other fist, I stopped it with my own to his face. It was more of a collision than a fight, and damn it, it's just the kind of stupid violence I hate — and *I* was doing it!"

A silence grew as he ran water over his hand at the sink. And then I did it, I spoke, "Well, you know, Ted. Sometimes you do have to break laws when the laws are wrong."

"What...?" This time it was Ted asking.

"Well, take Henry David Thoreau." I started in, "He says that when unjust laws exist we have three choices: to obey them and ignore the wrong; to continue to obey them and work to reform them; or we can 'transgress them at once' in an act of civil disobedience."

Ted was staring hard at me all the while I spoke. "Shut the fuck up, will you! I can't believe you're throwing this book shit at me. I never seen Thoreau on no picket line, and I sure as hell never seen him or you working no 3 to 11 shift."

"Wait a damn minute," I yelled, "This is not books talking; it's me, your brother."

"Then talk like my damn brother, will you, not some college Communist spouting crapola."

"This isn't communism, Ted; it's ethics and civil disobedience, just like your strikes. And where the hell did you get all this repressed anger, anyway?"

"Just, shut up, will you. Shut up!" He was really yelling now and shaking mad. "You go off to that damn college and come back thinking you're so much better than the rest of us. You forget where you come from, kid, who your family is, and most of all how to talk plain. I mean it, brother, you've *changed*."

That outburst blew me away for a couple of minutes. I felt like I'd just had the wind knocked out of me by my brother's bloody fist. I just stood there by the kitchen window asking who was this guy I was arguing with. Was this the same fellow who had pushed me all my life toward those college doors? "Do it, Marco, make something more of yourself. Make choices that matter. It's a degree that'll buy you freedom, and more security than I had at the mill or than I'll ever have at Ford." Ted had been my coach and mentor since high school, and before that when we were kids. He would come home from school, and we'd sit on the stairs before supper, and he'd teach me all that he'd learned that day. Christ, it was his voice inside my head. What had gone wrong? I was angry and sad and just *lost* inside an empty rage.

"See you," I said, and I walked right out the door and drove home in the rain. It was a long lonely drive that I needed. It felt like the end of something big. When I got home, I made coffee without thinking, sat at the table, and by the time it was coffee, there was Ted coming through the door. He walked right up to me.

"Marco, I'm sorry." He could always say those words first. "I'm sorry for all I said. Listen, kid, I love your going to college. It's a right thing for us all — I mean Mom and Pop too, even little JoAnn, they would all want it. I spoke...wrong."

"No, Ted, you're right about some of it. I do act like a smartass sometimes, throwing quotes from textbooks at you. Talking the talk of my teachers. I keep trying on new ideas like clothes, seeing what fits. And I am changing, man, in ways I don't even understand."

We were both speaking truth here that spread a quiet calm over the room. The cat ran from the couch into the bathroom. We looked up and I spoke plain, "Listen, Ted, you are always my brother. You and Margie and the kids are my only real family now, besides Maria. I would never ever put you down."

"I know that, little brother, believe me. And I know how hard you're working for all of us. So..." I looked into his eyes and shook that big broad hand of his.

And now standing here in their kitchen, looking at Ted in his old Browns T-shirt, I see this big shouldered brother of mine, and we both know something real, the work of speaking our love.

EATING AMERICAN PIE

Monday I start teaching at St. Mary's. Graduate on Friday—Start my first teaching job on Monday—pretty damn good, eh? Course, I'm leaving out the 30 years that brought me to this American dream pot. It's all a long story. Yet here I am in the midst of it, working out my lesson plans from these old textbooks: *An Appreciation of Literature* and *Perrin's Basic Grammar and Usage*. My students are supposed to learn how to write an essay, so I'm going to start them off with a family story: "Write a Story of One of Your Grandparents—250-300 words, double space, one side of the paper, please."

Sister Agnes explained that most of these kids are either from working class families who still have jobs at Ford or USS/KOBE Steel, or their folks are working in service areas. Some are the kids of doctors and lawyers living in the suburban neighborhoods along the edge of the city, afraid to send their kids to public schools. And some are from the great American underclass—children of the unemployed or single working mothers—taking Catholic scholarships to an education. I'm trusting that their grandparents are the common ground, because if you go back far enough, most of us here are tied to the work at the American Shipping Yards, the Lorain steel mills, the Ford plant, or to migrant labor. Lorain—The International City—Ethnic City—a regular tossed salad of fresh vegetables and aged spices. We'll see what these eighth graders find to tell.

I guess I'm thinking this way because of the commencement speaker at Ashland University yesterday. See, I took most of my courses here at Lorain Community College, but my degree comes through Ashland University, 50 miles south of here. They call it collaborative education, and I'm sure it's good business for both schools. I know it got me this far.

Yesterday we drove down early to Ashland to see the campus and find the gymnasium where I'd graduate.

Esther and Luis, Maria and I, drove around the campus without getting out of the car; then we found a Bob Evans Restaurant outside of town where we had lunch. Amidst the gingham and formica, Luis ordered eggs and bacon with biscuits and gravy. The rest of us ordered soup and sandwich specials.

Waiting for our food to arrive, Esther makes Luis tell the story of his coming to Ohio.

"That story is too long," Luis protests, "too long and far away now."

"Luis...Please," begs Esther leaning her face on his shoulder and tugging lightly on his arm.

"Okay, okay," he says, then drawing on his Winston, looks around and begins, "I tell just the story of Ohio." And he hesitates, "But first we go back to California to begin. We was working then, my family and me, in the fields picking avocadoes and peaches, Mendocino grapes and the San Diego tomatoes. We was getting along okay, my mother and father, my two brothers and three sisters. It was 1968, I remember because that year they shot Bobby Kennedy and Martin Luther King, and our soldiers was fighting in Vietnam. But for us Chicanos, it was the year of Cesar Chavez when suddenly the word Strike had meaning again. You know, this little guy, he come right out of the fields to speak for us. Kennedy and King both stood with him. I remember ...but that's another story." Luis takes a slow sip of his black coffee.

"Oh, we had the low pay, the shitty houses with the rats, the scorn of the owners who made us pay high for food and carry our water from irrigation ditches—and all their stupid curses were there for us. But, what was really killing us then was the sprays—new ones and more. They would spray the shit out of those fields one day, and the next we'd be out there picking them. Chemicals was a big thing in the sixties, and they sprayed us to death like it was the fields of Vietnam." He pauses and looks around. "Ahh...the times was bad and good. Bad for the sickness we was taking in, and good cause of the way we was fighting back. 'Ban the Grapes' was everywhere. The boycott was spreading. I mean we was marching then. Someone would pull up to a camp in a pickup, toot a horn, and twenty people would come out and jump into the back. We'd drive off to the big cities. In San Francisco they cheered us in the streets. In Sacramento they spit in our faces, called us the names. Some said we was 'un-American,' cause we struck during a war. What did they know about wars? We carried on."

"How did you get by during the strike," Maria asks.

Luis looks up, "We got by. There was some help come in from the other unions, but it didn't last, and pretty soon we was almost starving. The little ones would be hungry and ask for food, and the men would have to get up and go outside. But Chavez he was there with us, going around to each camp, and so he knew, and what he did was he went into a fast—refused to eat till something was done. He found strength in starving himself. I met him once in San Jose, a really gentle man. I can't believe the pictures now...how small he looks, when he was so big to us. He spoke up for us all, so that finally we were heard."

Luis grinds out his cigarette in the ashtray. He is more animated than I have ever seen him. He reads our faces, "You see, it's a long story, and I'm not even to Ohio." He looks over at the waitress bringing on our platters of food. Luis smiles at her, "Gracias," he says.

"Grato," she returns. "Hey, how'd you know I was Chicano?" Luis has a way of watching people, a close eye and ear for things.

"A girl as pretty as you...?" he says, and she laughs.

"What brings you into town, amigos?" she asks.

Esther smiles, "Marco here" pointing to me with her spoon, "is graduating today from Ashland University. He's my son-in-law."

I grin, and Maria reaches over to rustle my hair, "I'm his wife Maria. And this is my step-dad Luis."

"Congratulations, to all of you," she smiles pretty and steps back. "Can I get you anything else?"

"No, I don't think so," I say, but Luis orders another bowl of gravy and biscuits for us all to have a bite.

For a moment we all look back to our storyteller. Luis tilts his head, spreads his hands, and says, "Let's eat."

While we wait for our check, I ask Luis, "You know, you never got to Ohio. Can you give us the rest of the story now?"

"Marco," he speaks softly, looking around. "This is the part of the story that can't be spoken in a place like this. We'll speak more in the car."

We were only a few blocks from the college gymnasium where we had to go, so I begged him to tell us there in the Bob Evans parking lot.

"No, you drive, I make it simple," he says from the passenger seat. "Anyway in the strike camps, people get hungry, and pretty soon some of those people, they cross the picket lines. But not me, not this time. And one night on the road to a vineyard I am standing on the picket line with my two brothers. It is dark, and we are telling stories around a barrel of fire, when suddenly we look up at two headlights from a big truck. The lights get bigger so fast we can't move, and then we are sent flying everywhere, us and the burning barrel into the fields. We just lie there. And then they make a mistake, because these two guys get out to see if we are dead. We are not. Some of our bones are broken, but we are not dead, just lying there waiting." Suddenly Luis looks around at Esther in the back seat, "What you say? Can I tell them this?"

She must have nodded, because then he adds, "One of those guys lying in the field, the one who could still get up, he waits with his face in the mud, and then when they are not looking, he picks up a burning two-by-four, and he slams it into one guy's back. There is much yelling and the other one turns to catch another blow. All the time, the man doing this is remembering Cesar Chavez asking us not to use violence, to endure for what is right. And so that night, no one is beaten to death, only three brothers end up helping some guys' truck drive over a cliff. Then we brothers climb back into our little car and..."

"What, Luis?" asks Maria from the back seat. "What?"

Luis only smiles as we pull into the parking lot, "And then, amigos, we drive to Ohio."

At the gymnasium I find seats for them in the fifth row. Ted and Marge are driving down separately, and so we save seats on the aisle. To tell the truth, I would just as soon they had missed it. The speaker is this former ambassador to Greece under Nixon, Wilfred Taylor. He wrote a book *American Values,* and he works now for the Hoover Foundation, a regular stink tank.

It is the school's fall semester graduation, so not many are picking up their sheep skin, and we graduates all get to sit up on the stage. I am all dressed in black robe with that mortar board hat and gold tassel bobbing in my face, like you see in the movies. What is nice is how I can see Maria's round face in the fifth row smiling back at me like a sun through trees. Luis is dressed in his western suit with a string tie, and Esther wears a bright flowered dress. Afterward she will kiss me and whisper, "Someday you can tell your baby he was here when his papa graduated." That's what I'll remember most in the long of it—having family there with me. But right now my head is still full of anger at that Taylor fellow's speech.

He starts off with that American melting pot theory—that we're all one big soupy mass here in "This great country of ours where class does not and need not exist." This naturally brings on applause. I watch Maria's face wrinkle like she'd bit a lemon. Ted and Marge are there by then, and he just stares back into Taylor's face. "Do not be led into division, my friends, by those who seek a multi-America. Beware the advocates of something called cultural diversity and an American pluralism. We are one...One nation, under God, **indivisible** with liberty and justice for all." That's what he says, I swear it, and the gymnasium just echoes with dumb applause. It is that old sermon of 'classlessness,' the same one that keeps the lights off and the shades drawn in our American house. As professor Santangello asked us once, "If you can't see the problem, then how can you fix it?" I lay my cane across my lap and rock back and forth.

"*Class*, my friends, is only a mask, something you must throw off as we all move together to the great middle." I look out at Luis' face and wonder what Taylor would make of his story this morning, or of Grandma Lorenz's American story. When she was in the third grade her teacher, Mrs. Walker, used to come into the room, sniff a few times, then make the Italian kids leave one by one while she searched for the one with the odor. "She was a regular witch," Grandma said once, "She didn't know how much that hurt us or how it made us stick together. So that one day Lucy Carocci and Dominic Caputto, they brought in some big cloves of garlic and stuffed them inside the air registers. Ah Dio, how her face wrinkled up walking around that room! 'Alright, who did it?' she asked, and we all held up our hands. Finally she got one of the American kids to tell who it was, and they both were paddled." Grandma Lorenz's face would be smiling, "I never told you, and I hate to say it, but I hated that woman for what she done to us. We was little kids, see, but we showed her, we stood up."

Remembering this helps me get through the rest of that speech, because, like anyone with their lights on, I know that class does exist in America and that people have suffered long through it. Taylor's asking them to ignore their life stories was like cutting off their faces, like forcing them to drink scalding hot soup from that old melting pot. They were never accepted into the American middle class, nor were they asking to be. It was all a lie that allowed people to be *marginalized* — a college word I picked up in a women's studies course. It explains how the names of people I loved were being written in tiny print in the margins of a page of America — there but not essential — and one day we knew their names would be dropped off the page.

Taylor was into his testimonial, "Friends, I did it my way, the American way. We're all equal here." He was telling the story of his father's selling insurance to Blacks and Chicanos. "My father went right into these peoples' homes." Then we hear how he graduates from college and serves as a lieutenant in Vietnam. "I came home wounded and became an Ohio congressman, proudly serving my state and country." Finally Nixon appoints him ambassador to Greece.

"We can all do this. All it takes is determination in this great nation of ours—the home of the brave, the land of the free." Ted gets up at that point, and I think he might speak out, but he just rises, looks into Taylor's red face, turns and walks out the central aisle. I tell you I loved his broad shouldered back stretching his suit coat as he moved down the aisle. Taylor just kept talking. He needs to believe his words.

It's not that we don't believe in such things as *equality* and *freedom* and *acceptance*, we do, but we also know that pretending it is so when it isn't is part of the chains we all wear. Ted came back when they started to read off the names, and we nodded together as he sat down by Marge. Oh yeah, when they spoke my name and I rose, my little group clapped and cheered, even though we were told to hold our applause till the end. We had been holding our applause for decades. It was time to make some sounds.

That evening we drove all the way back to El Patio in South Lorain. Ted had the little band play an Italian polka, and all of us danced and sang and ate the food of Americans.

This week we'll see what American stories my students bring in to tell.

DEPENDING ON IT

    Maria and I talked about my buying a beeper in case she goes into labor while I am at work. We couldn't afford it anyway until after my first paycheck. For now we'll trust the school's secretary to reach me by messenger, and Maria has a backup system in her mom and of course Margaret. Now Maria can see that I am having trouble with leaving her for this first day of teaching, so she comes over and she leans against me. "Don't you worry, Hon," she says placing my hands on her soft hips, "I'm not having this baby without you at my side."
    So I check my backpack again for the essentials, grab my brown bag lunch, and kiss Maria one more time. She tastes of eggs and toast, her hair of moist flowers. I'll admit, as I close the door and head down the steps, I feel the hot sting of tears.
    I arrive at St. Mary's parking lot at seven a.m. School begins at seven thirty. There is a nice crispness in the air, as I stand at the playground fence breathing it in. The lot is empty and for the first time quiet. Lights are coming on in the huge apartment building across the street. I would lock my car door if the latches weren't still busted. Someone broke in and stole Maria's purse last Sunday. It was hidden under the seat, so they must have been watching as she got out. She lost her identifications and a rosary her grandmother gave her. I mean, Christ, a pregnant woman going to church, and someone robs her. She cried off and on most of that Sunday.
    I enter the building through the back door. It smells warm, and the lights are calling me awake. I walk the hallway slowly, like I'm watching myself in slow motion. Okay, maybe I am thinking about how I'll write all this down in this journal during lunch. I can't help feeling the momentum of all this, yet what I'm drawn to here is my life. I stand outside room 237 for a minute, look through the glass win-

dow in the door. I push past the dark wood of the doorway—all the years of teaching and learning that have gone on in this space. I remember Professor Watson warning, "Don't ever forget that teaching and learning are not the same...related but not the same. See it from their heads and hearts." This morning I hope they'll be willing to see it from mine.

    I lay out my things, then take my lunch down to the faculty lounge where I meet an older woman. She is someone I think I have seen around Lorain, maybe at the Deli. She rises from her chair, "Good morning, I'm Helen Heinz, eighth grade math." She extends her small hand, "And you are..."

    "Marco Lorenz," I say too softly.

    "Sorry, son. You'll have to speak up. I've been teaching a long time."

    "**Marco-Lorenz**," I say too loud.

    "Welcome, Mr. Lorenz, to St. Mary's school." She smiles nicely, "I hope you have a good year with us." She sees my lunch bag and opens the refrigerator— "Let me make some space for your lunch in here."

    I hand her my sack, and she looks down at it, "Son, you'd better put your name on that." And I look into a refrigerator full of bags of all sizes, no school cafeteria at St. Mary's.

    "Gotcha," I say.

    "Gotcha?" she repeats, as I take out my pen. "Isn't it English you're teaching, Mr. Lorenz?"

    "Yes, it is, Mrs. Heinz," I report.

    "Well, I'd advise you that students learn more from your example than your lessons." She pauses then lets out a sigh and pats my arm, "Oh, I'm sorry for that; first days are hard...and everyday has its struggle. I don't mean to add to yours." I begin to see the light of concern in her eyes; how else could she teach and survive?

    "It's alright," I say, "And please call me Marco."

    "You'll do fine," she says finally and for the first time I begin to realize that I might not. Desire only gets you to the door. "Now, if you can stand one more bit of advice," she is at the door, "Start out on firm ground, Marco. It's easier to relax later than to tighten up." I am still looking a little puzzled, so she adds, "It's hard to drive a car with loose steering," and disappears.

 I sit on the leather couch. Outside come the first yells of children on the playground. I look down at my new shoes and wonder just how deep are these waters that I'm stepping into.

 By the time the 7:20 bell has rung bringing in the students, I have filled one board with a poem and begun to write an assignment when I realize that we start the day with home room. The students rush in, most at the last minute, all in fresh looking uniforms—the girls in the blue plaid jumpers and white blouses, the boys in white shirts, blue ties and slacks. They are dressed better than I am in my blue denim shirt and black tie. Another thing I'm buying after my first check is a sports coat. The faces bubble about as in boiling water. I stand before them and wait for their quiet. Some stare back at me, others begin laughing. My hand sneaks down to check my fly—okay there. *What's up?* is written across my face. Finally a tall girl in the front row whispers, "You're supposed to be calling roll." She is right, and I begin to do so when the voice of Sister Agnes comes over the speaker with the morning's announcements. Mary Kelley leads us in the day's prayer.

 "Okay," I say after the A-men, "I'm Mr. Lorenz. All those not here please raise your hands." It earns me my first smile. "Don't worry. I'll get it right tomorrow." The bell rings, and I yell over the roar, "Have a good day, Homeroom 237."

 Slowly and with some flutter my first class begins filing in. As they take their seats I check to see that I have the right books, am in the right classroom. Yes, and I have Sister Anne's seating chart to guide me. She has seated them boy-girl, boy-girl and put little checks by the "talkers." I took this to be a mark of eagerness, yet looking out at the faces, I realize it indicates those who need to be watched. Anyway it's hard to go by another person's map.

"Students, please," my voice tries to rise above the chatter. "Students, I am Mr. Marco Lorenz, your English instructor." They do not quiet, and I begin to feel I must make an example of someone, when, like magic, a second bell rings and they are all quiet and facing front. There are rules inside of rules. I begin again.

I give them some background on myself and family, that I am from Lorain, that my leg was injured in a strike, that I will not hit them with my cane. They listen and look around—"What to make of this guy?" I notice a red haired girl by the windows smiles, the one who bumped into me in the hall the other day. I look down: Laura McDonald, no check mark.

I begin moving to the board where I hear myself say, "Okay, students of eighth grade English, let's start this journey of ours. We'll begin with a writing assignment." Quiet waits as I scroll on the board: "Write a family story of one of your grandparents. It may be one they tell or one that is told about them. 250 to 300 words in ink, double spaced, one side of the paper please. Due Monday, November 19th." There is an audible groan, and I turn. One boy seated by the window is visibly distressed. I check the chart: Mario DiCarlo, a check. "Mario, do you want to tell us how you feel about this?"

"Yeah, Father, I'll tell you."

"He's not a priest," someone whispers.

"Oh, sorry, Mr. Lorenzo," he grins back.

"Mr. Lorenz, Mario," I correct. "You were going to tell us how you feel about the assignment."

"Well, it's like this," he grins and takes his thumb and finger and pinches them right over his nostrils. Laughter.

I can't help grinning myself. "And the rest of you? How do your feel about this?"

In a surprise stroke of unity all of them lift their hands to their noses, and it looks like a tour of a slaughter house. I laugh and someone yells, "Who cut the cheese?" and there's another roar. The words "Start on firm ground" rise to my head, but I am enjoying this, so I let it pass.

Though surprised by their resistance, I am still prepared. I pass out xerox copies of an essay entitled, "Growing Up Polish in Pittsburgh."

"We'll share a little reading here that might help you. No, it's not in your books," and I pass out the rest of my copies run at Kinko's two days ago. It is by Carolyn Banks, and is the kind of writing I want to do someday...close and deep inside yet light outside. Inside the laughter there is love. It begins:

> The section of the city was called "Polish Hill." It consisted of narrow streets and row houses, brick pavements gradually being replaced by concrete and sidewalks. A few flat fences were left, but these, too, were going, and in their stead, aluminum chain-link fences were being raised.

Each student reads a paragraph at a time and we talk and explain. And so we move with the author from the market to the church with its morning Masses and its plaster Saints. We climb about the hill with Carolyn and her mother and her Aunt Clara, *babkas* in *babushkas*. At the church bingo Aunt Clara wins a toaster. Some of the students tell bingo or aunt stories of their own. And then we share the night Aunt Clara saw the vision of the Virgin and the whole neighborhood came out.

> A fire engine appeared, quite suddenly. It came slowly, as fire trucks driven in parades, but with its headlights on, the fire bell clanging. A man called through a megaphone, "Go home, go home. There is nothing here to see." And someone shouted, "Protestant!" The crowd laughed and cheered and applauded.

And so do my students, moved by the way writing can still touch us. "This," I dare to say, "is a family story. Talk with your parents or grandparents if you're lucky enough to still have them. Don't make things up. Tell a story that is true."

There are a few questions, "How long does it have to be? When is it due?" Though I have this written on the board, I repeat it while I collect the story copies for the next class. I am ready to dismiss them when I look up — there are ten minutes still in the period. What to do? I do what any good teacher would, I set them to work on the assignment. "Begin working on this at your desk. Sketch out a few ideas. Raise your hand if you need some help." They take out paper and stare at it... Then Laura McDonald raises her hand. Pointing to the poem on the board she asks, "Mr. Lorenz, is that for us?"

Ah, yes, the poem, I had forgotten. "Well, yes, it's the poem for the day. Each day I plan to write a poem on that board. Let's read it together today. It is by Dr. William Carlos Williams, a pediatrician from New Jersey:

THE RED WHEELBARROW

so much depends
upon

a red wheel
barrow

glazed with rain
water

beside the white
chickens

I read it, then we read it together. My feeling of satisfaction is shattered by Mario's voice, "I don't get it. I don't. What's it supposed to mean...a red wheelbarrow and some chickens? Is that a poem?"

"Yes," is all I have time to reply before the bell. "And you *all* are glazed wheelbarrows and white chickens," I add as they begin filing out. Some are smiling, others are shaking their heads, and I turn to my desk to prepare to do this whole thing again four more times. There stand two students, my red haired girl and a small dark haired girl.

"Mr. Lorenz," Laura speaks softly. "Can we ask you something?"

"Sure."

"Well...Would it be okay someday if we brought in our own poems?"

"That would be great," I smile inside and out, feeling blessed. She smiles and runs along.

The other girl stays behind. I see on the chart that her name is Sonia Mendozza, no check. "Yes, what is it?" I ask looking down into her dark eyes which she turns from me.

"Do we have to share them with the class?" she asks above a whisper.

"The poems or the stories?"

"The stories I mean, Mr. Lorenz. I don't want to read mine out loud. Okay?"

"Of course," I smile, though my face must seem as much a question to her as hers is to me. I check the clock. A fresh bunch of students come streaming in. "You'd better go, Sonia, or you'll be late."

"That's okay, I don't really care," she says and is gone.

MILKING IT

9 p.m. my schoolwork done, I look up from the kitchen table over to Maria on the couch. I want to ask her what she thinks of dark eyed Sonia's question, but I can tell Maria is in a bad mood and does not want to talk. When I move over beside her on the couch, she turns away.

"What's wrong, Baby?" I ask softly stroking her arm. Her dark hair is so sleek and long.

"Nothing," she sighs. "Just nothing at all," and she begins to cry gently. I have learned not to push at these times. I move my hand up her arms and begin rubbing her shoulders and neck.

"No, that's enough," she says pulling away, and I am lost in the dark forest of her feelings.

I ask directions, "Do you want to tell me about it?"

She takes a tissue form her sweater pocket, wipes her eyes, turning her face from side to side in a woman's way. "Okay, Marco. I'll tell you, but you have to just listen...Do you hear—just *listen* to me."

"Go ahead," I say. "I'll listen."

"Well, first of all, I know I'm a fat blob...an ugly sack of potatoes."

I hold back.

"I'm as ugly as sin, a real swollen toad face. I know."

"Maria, you're beaitful."

"Marco...just listen, *please*. I need you to *listen*. I don't sleep at night, and in the day I can't get off this couch. I'm always tired, tired, tired. I swear I am stuck in a hole, in a deep hole of nothingness."

I don't speak.

"Just look at me. Look! How could anyone stand being near me? I know I can't."

"But, I love you, Maria. You look..."

"Damn it, Marco," her face is red and tight. "Are you going to listen or what? Oh, just shut up." She starts to cry again, then tries to rise from the couch but cannot.

I hold her by the wrist, "Don't leave, Maria. Go on. I'll listen."

"No, you don't understand. I have to get up. Look... Look..." She looks down at the wet circles on her red blouse and begins to cry harder. Her neck is shaking with each sob. "Oh, God," she sighs, "I'm leaking all over the place."

I follow her into the bedroom, sit on the bed as she stands before the mirror. She removes her wet blouse, her large white bra, and stands there naked to the waist. She is an earth mother, I swear it, her tan skin so full and lovely. I want to tell her this, kiss her nakedness...but do not.

She is wiping herself, looking into the mirror, slowly examining her plump raspberry nipples. "Oh, Marco, I'm so tender." She tosses me a look and a box. "Open these for me, please."

This is new to me, "Nursing Pads?"

"Yes, the clinic nurse gave them to me, remember?" I try to tear open the clear plastic bag, finally bite it with my teeth. I touch the soft cottony pads, place them into Maria's open hand. She examines them a moment, then lays them one at a time across each nipple area. She pulls her bra cups up and around; then begins to latch herself, but turns slowly to face me. "Oh, Marco, I have to prepare my nipples for the baby. I need you to...to milk me." I lie back on the bed amazed and already feeling a flame rising from my groin. "That one nurse at the clinic, she said I should pinch them to get them ready, but I've tried and I can't." Maria looks deep into my eyes, "My mother said that you should suck them for me." She is a dark goddess coming towards me. I sit up, embrace her waist, my head touching her strong yet tender stomach, "Please... Marco...could you...*please*..."

I am walking on water here, one doubt will sink me. I nod slowly. Her straps fall down like rose petals. She carefully lifts off the pads and we begin a ritual dance, rocking in slow motion, sucking the sweet, warm and milky liquid of this life between us. It is an act of woman and man as old as love and birth.

READING PAPERS

Of my students papers many are fine. They tell the stories of families, of how brave grandparents came here for work, how they met and started families in this place. Many of these students speak their love for a grandparent who cared for them and now is gone. I get excited about many and read parts of them to Maria. Yet there is one paper that is remarkable, and, yes, it is the paper of Sonia Mendozza.

I come upon it halfway through my 8 o'clock set. In a carefully written hand it begins, "It is hard for me to write the truth here. Telling the truth is one of the greatest struggles of my life. I know that telling it causes pain. And so to stop the beatings by my mother, I have learned to lie. I lie so well now I cannot tell the truth for myself. With each word, each sentence here, I fear I will begin to lie again. I cannot stop it, because, though my mother still beats me often, she cannot beat away my need for her love."

I sit up from the couch. These words come bleeding from the pages onto my hands. I look out the window's darkening light toward the trees and street, take another drink of coffee and continue.

"I remember when my brother Jose was born. My sister Nitta and I, we were swept away to a neighbor's house. Mama drove off with Papa, and in secrecy we waited in an old man's house. I remember staring at the old rags stuffed into his cold windows and feeling shame. Something was wrong with me so deep I couldn't cry."

I set down my pen. How can I begin to mark such a paper? I look around. Maria is sleeping softly in the other room; I cannot wake her. And so I read on alone.

"And then one fall day walking home from school, I suddenly ran across the street for no reason and was struck by a car. I remember being picked up by a man. He laid me down on a back seat and drove me to St. Joseph's Hospital. I watched the trees pass through the windows as we drove down the street. Inside the building we learned that my arm was broken in a bad place, at the wrist. I lay in the hospital on the white sheets for two days. My mother came and went, and I kept looking out the window and waiting.

"When I went home, I found I had my mother back again. She would come and comfort me. She would bring me things to eat. I can still see her sitting in a chair or lying beside me in my bed talking to me, listening, feeding me chicken-rice soup. It was painful to get well. My suffering had brought me love. I became a sickly child."

Reading this I try to see Sonia's face again — those dark eyes and braided hair. How old can she be — thirteen at most? In class she is always looking down or away. Once I saw her reading another book as I talked. When I called on her, she answered correctly without looking up. She is never talking with the others or running through the halls. Always her movement is slow and secretive. Yet somehow already this child has learned how words can speak for her.

"I write this here so you will know how much pain it causes me to tell the truth. It is not as easy as you say to 'Just be honest. Write your life.' It causes some great pain, and yet I want desperately to tell what is true. I fear that otherwise I will lose myself and disappear into a world of lies. I know this paper is not what you asked us for, but I'm trying to get to that. Mr. Lorenz, I have no grandparents to write of. They were left in Mexico long before I was born. My mother never speaks of them. And once I heard my father yelling at my mother that he was cheated when he bought her. I know that they were poor as poor. Only my mother's mother still lives, a face I've never seen but whose cruelty to my mother I know has come down to me. Once my mother called me 'mugre' (filth) and made me go into the yard and eat dirt. 'I give you some of my mother's black medicine,' she said and slammed the back door. So I can only begin with my own mother, the story of Rosa Chichu, this woman from Zamora, who married my father Juan Mendozza from Arandas. They came to America and one day in 1980 followed the migrant work north into Lorain County. Three years later they had the ugly child who is me."

I quickly leaf through the pages—three more. This girl writes so straight of life and cuts so deeply somehow opening the heart in a way I have only begun to.

"When I asked myself how my mother could beat me, her child, slap my face with an open hand or a closed fist, beat my bare butt with my father's old leather belt, my answer was always the same—my unworthiness, my brutishness. I was nothing and she was everything to me. I see now that my need for her love gave her that power. I knew it even then when I felt it could not change. And then one day the perfection shattered. My father was away picking in the West. He had been gone for a month. On Sundays he would call and speak only to my mother. She would tell us, 'Your father is alright. He is in California till February.' That was my birthday month. He was always home by then. When my father was here with us, my mother never beat us, though she would call us ugly names in front of him.

"And then while he was gone my mother began answering the phone in secret. We children were sent out of the house, 'Go on. Out! Sit on the porch. Out. Out!' she would shout. No matter how we were dressed, we were thrown out. I once sat out there in my slip for an hour hiding in a corner, praying no one would come knocking on our door. Mother's secrets were pushing us out the door. Then one night I saw them, her and this dark man in a pick-up truck. It was late and we were all in bed. I was still awake reading when I heard an engine and looked out. He turned his lights off and on, off and on, and then she went out to him. I could see from my window. At first I thought it could be my father, so I snuck down. I looked out the front window and saw them—kissing wildly in the truck, rubbing their hands in each other's hair. Oh how I hated her then! She had lied and cheated, and she had broken her own spell over me. I went back upstairs and I cried and I cursed her. She had torn herself from me. I lay in bed there a half person. I stared out at the night for hours till I finally fell asleep.

"Mr. Lorenz, this is my awful story of my broken family and of my mother and me. I could not tell it another way because I am still that half person that you see."

This paper is too much. It shakes in my hand as I walk into the bedroom and begin rubbing Maria's sleeping arm, "Maria, wake up. Maria, please. I need to read you something."

HOUSING

    Maria and I talk of Sonia Mendozza, of what her life must be like. We think hard of what we might do to help her, of what we must. And then we sleep. Soon Maria wakes up in the night. She is having trouble sleeping with the baby coming, "I can't find the right position," she says, and I hear in her voice *a future* and *a now* that echo my own. This baby is coming towards us, yet is with us everywhere.

    I am up now with Maria, only she fell back to sleep on the couch. I rubbed her feet and listened while she told me how she felt, and that has put her back to sleep, like a child.
    It's now 5 a m, Wednesday morning here in Lorain. I can hear the clock ticking, the faucet dripping. I have no answers for little Sonia, and I realize also that I have not written anything but lesson plans for days. So with Maria's soft breathing beside me, I pick up my pen and I write. And what I come to write of is *women*, how they are *houses* we men live outside. There is Maria's body so near me already giving home to our child. An hour ago she told me through tears, "Marco, I don't know how I'll part with it. Like no other, this child shares my place. We are the same body." A man hears these things and he knows, but he cannot realize. He may even understand somehow, but forever he remains outside where he is always building a place to house his family.

    I see now my mother and father and the way this was in their lives. Dad worked at the mills, long hours and in shifts, "bringing home the bacon," he used to say. Or he would stop at Avante's Bakery and buy a fresh loaf of Italian bread just so he could place it on the table hard and announce, "Well, here is your daily bread, family." And he was also there for house repair—the ones he could handle, like painting and raking and putting up drain spouts or hanging a door, and the ones he could not: the plumbing and wiring, repairing washers and dryers. There he would start and make worse. Curses would rise from the basement or garage, "Damn, damn, damn, damn, damn"—He always cursed in fives. Finally a repairman would be called in. When he arrived, Dad would be outside doing something on the car. He'd coach Mom or one of us kids on how to explain the problem, because he didn't want to be there when the repairman asked his questions, "Has someone been messing with this?" No, Dad was no expert, but he was our provider.

Mom, on the other hand, *was the house*. I know women today hate the term "housewife," and I can understand it, but to me Mom *was* the house. It was her body as well as her domain, and any part violated brought screams of personal pain, "Aak!" she would cry, "Who tracked mud onto my carpet?" And we would all look quick at who wore the guilty shoes. Once she woke me an hour early for school so I'd have time to put away my things. "We each do our part," she would say, and we would nod, but mostly we did not...do our part. It was she who took in the slack for us all. She who kept surfaces clear on tables and counters, removed the rubble from floors and stairs. And we became part of the house she cared for like her own body.

In the midst of poverty and filth—the mills spilling ore and coal dust onto everything each day—she swept. She was the cleanest woman alive. "Mrs. Clean," I once heard a neighbor woman call her. That day she had been sweeping the porch and taken it out into the yard where she began sweeping the grass—I swear it. One day she cut down our favorite maple tree, said, "Its leaves make nothing but filth."

Inside the house her urge for cleanliness knew no ends. The smell of vinegar and Clorox fought with any aromas of sauerkraut and sausage. Each year she would repaint her kitchen with another coat of white glossy paint till the paint wouldn't stick anymore and had to be scraped. Our clothes weren't often new, but they had to be clean especially if we went out. "Don't you step a foot out that door in those dirty pants." Our underwear was, of course, kept both clean and new for any trips to the emergency room.

As kids we just figured Mom was a little nuts. Yet we'd take pride at times when our friends were impressed. Finding her cleaning down the wall paper with that green clayey stuff, they would ask, "What the heck's your mom doing?" And we would act smartass and explain, "Oh she's just cleaning the clean." And Mom never wasted anything either. Leftovers were a way of life in our family, but you had to call them "casseroles," or you wouldn't eat. Some nights in the kitchen you'd find her going through a basket of clothes; her lips would be pursed and her eyes open wide through the glasses. She'd be making piles of what we could still wear, what needed mending, and what were now the rags and rummage. It was a close call week to week.

We did not understand Mom nor her compulsion to save or keep clean. We just watched it like a game. And then one Sunday the family was out for a ride. I remember we were driving past a row of shacks by the tracks, out by the old nut and washer plant. Dad slowed to a stop and asked, "Hey, Mother, didn't you once live there?" Mom's cheeks flushed and her head went down. She didn't need to answer. As we passed we all gawked out at the place — piles of trash thrown along the side wall, shingles torn off the sides, a dirt yard with a front stoop of rotted wooden stairs. I remember Ted exclaimed, "And I thought *we* were poor!" But me, I looked over at Mom and out of my big mouth came the words: "You lived *there!*"

"Yes," was all she ever said, without raising her head, as we drove on in silence like we'd just been to a home funeral.

I was around 13 then, and I remember thinking on the ride home how it must have felt being a kid from a dump like that. When I asked Dad about it in the garage, he just said, "Your mother's family was poor, really poor. In the time when I first knew her in high school they lived in a dozen such places. They was always moving ahead of the back rent, you understand?" He could read the pain in my eyes, and so he added, "Her folks was good people, boy, just rough and forever down on their luck. Your Mom never had a thing till we married and rented our first place, a garage apartment over on Clifton Street. I was working the track gang then, making minimum, but in a week she turned those two little rooms into a home. Listen son, your Mom's a good woman all her life. Remember that." It was the most I heard him speak of her like that ever.

    I sat in my room thinking of her as a person like me. She needed her space too, one that was clean and safe and her own. She'd been making homes wherever she'd gone. I sat there a long time, and then I went down to the kitchen and I had a big bowl of Cheerios. I watched Mom moving around, wiping circles on the refrigerator and stove. "Be sure to clean up when you're done, son," she said.

    "I will," I said without looking up.

COUNTING OUR LOSSES

This morning I drive down Oberlin Avenue, and for some reason turn down 21st Street to my old neighborhood. In the dawn light of 7 a.m. I still have a half hour before my St. Mary's classes begin.
They have closed Marzetti's Grocery store for good. Someone has ripped off the old Wonder Bread screen door—I mean literally ripped it off its hinges and left it lying in a shambles by the steps. The economy takes its bite out of everything. Even the IGA that probably drove Marzetti's into bankruptcy is now talking of closing down. They can't compete with the new Meijer's Superstore out on route 58.
I pull up to the curb at Washington, our old house. I sit there letting the car's idle rock me. Got to get Ted to tune up this old heap if I want to make it through the year. The old house seems to be losing some of its shingles. God, how I hated those old pebbly things. "Surrounded by asphalt," we used to joke, except for the front porch where tan permastone sheets greeted us with old worn faces. I used to think it was real brick until Ted busted a sheet with his head in a fight with Dad about wrecking the old Dodge. I can still hear them yelling at each other, Ted in his school jacket, Dad in his work pants and t-shirt, both of them waving their arms, Mom pacing inside, and then Wham! Ted went up against the house. Mom screamed and tore open the door, then ran back into the house coming back from the kitchen with a bowl of water. She threw it on both of them, a quick spray that stunned them to a stop. They looked back, and she grabbed and pulled them into the hall. "You're acting like animals, both of you, out there in the street, for everyone to see. I won't have it!" Mom was so weak yet at times she could pull this power from somewhere deep inside her.
Both Dad and Ted stood back watching. It was like she'd already been there, done that, and just wouldn't have any more. And so Dad went back out to survey the dam-

ages, while I helped Ted wash off his bleeding head. I remember Dad talking to himself when he came in, "God Almighty, how are we going to pay for this? God Almighty, help us." I don't remember how we ever did pay for it, cause back then there was no emergency fund for anything. No backup, no reserve, and no one to borrow it from. Everything just hit us like a storm.

    I look down the street now at all these houses, worn out and about to go back to the earth. How long does a house have to live in old Lorain anyway? What are its chances for a long life in a city that's dying?

    I look around once and ease into traffic, time to be getting to work. I pass a couple kids in St. Mary's uniforms, one is punching the other in the arm in some kind of caveman game men play. I toot the horn and they stop.

    At the school parking lot, I can hear the organ music from the Mass being said. For now I'm okay with or without it, the mass that is, but I admit it's kind of nice, like chanting in the predawn dark. I'm starting to feel a little guilty about not going to Mass for so long. I don't know, I think I *think* too much. Sometimes the best way to do anything is just to do it...just a mindless sweeping without thought. What was it Dad used to say? "The best talking is not talking." Well, that's my meditation — Do what is there.

    Inside the building it is quiet, and I have brought with me my students' family essays. Yesterday in the faculty lounge I was wondering just how to return them. Helen Heinz suggested, "Wait till the end. Right away hold them up, then announce that you'll be returning them at the end of the period. It keeps their attention and protects you from too much complaining." The other faculty talked it over and agreed. In teaching, it's the little things that are big.

    I have marked some papers that I'd like returned so that I can make copies to share with the class. There is Antonio's story of his grandmother's coming over from Italy twice before she met and married a *cumpadre* from her native Giullianova. Susan Cowell's story was of her grandfather's working on the shipyards for thirty years till it shut down. He was jobless two years till he became this school's janitor. He told her, "What else should I do? I love my work, and it loves me back." Sonia Mendozza's paper is not one of them, yet it is clearly the most powerful. For comments I was reduced to such things as "Good clear voice...Moving details... Tight and to the point... Connect things here a little more." I did allow myself the praise, "This is fine writing, Sonia. You have a gift. Thanks for sharing so much of yourself here." Yet, I'm not sure that is true—her story cost me some sleep and has given me some haunting images. Her pain makes my own echo. When Maria and I read it the second time, we agreed to add, "Let's talk if you need help dealing with any of this." I'm uncertain, but Maria says that her friend Sylvia over at the Giving House will help talk with Sonia. I know something has to be done.

At first period, the students flow in, "Hey, got our papers?" asks Antonio.

"Yes, I have your papers, Antonio. We'll get to that." I am still matching faces with names—all 110 of my students. Laura has come in and is writing her poem on the board. Finally they sit down...but someone is missing—Sonia Mendozza. "Settle down," I repeat. "Does anyone know where Sonia is?"

Kari answers first, "She's not here anymore. I think she moved away."

Another shouts, "No, I heard she had to drop out." It is as though someone has punched the air out of my lungs—another fistful of loss. I gasp twice quietly, turn around, and walk slowly to the board where I read Laura's chalked poem:

> MY FRIENDS
> Someone has reached out
> and touched me to my heart.
> Someone has opened me
> and I pray we'll never part.
> Bright threads around hands
> weave a circle of friends.

I turn back to the class, "Okay," I say hard, "Get out your grammar and usage books. Today we're going to work on fragments."

GETTING THE WORD

I drive the long way home from school, out along North Ridge Road. At the McDonalds drive-thru I get a cup of black coffee, burn my mouth sipping it, bring on stinging tears.

Why is there always something hurting me and those I care for? I'm into a blaming mood—being the victim, because I'm poor, disabled, from an abandoned city along a wounded lake. I know this leads nowhere, that I have to quit blaming a system outside of myself—government, politics, education, the economy, racism, sexism. I've worked this all out in sessions with Dr. Atkins. When I make it something *out there*, it's not me, and I can't begin to deal with it as the real fear and pain I carry around inside. I understand all this, I do, and still there is all this social pain that's so damn real.

Little Sonia is gone, like that, like a starling flown out of the yard, and there seems nothing I can do. This morning when I talked with Sister Agnes during my third period break, she stood there by her desk in a tight suit and declared bluntly, "Sonia Mendozza is no longer a student at St. Mary's School. She has been withdrawn by mutual consent."

"But whose?" I asked. "Whose consent?"

"That isn't your concern, Mr. Lorenz."

"Yes it is," I insisted. "She's my student."

"Not any more," she answered. And we stood squared off while she read the sharp lines in my face. "Her mother and I feel that Sonia should withdraw from St. Mary's and get some treatment at a public school. They have the funds and programs for that."

"Oh, please, Sister. We know how much those schools don't have. And the first person who needs the treatment here is the mother. Sonia needs our help."

I watched her neck and head flinch as she turned, "I don't know what she told you, Mr. Lorenz, but I'll share this much. Sonia is a troubled student with a troubled past. She came here with a long record of lies, deceits, and dismissals. We are the third school she's attended in the last two years, and that is only because Father McNeil made hers a special case."

"But she is—a special case, Sister, because she's a child and a victim." I wondered how far I should go, but I knew this was Sonia's last chance at St. Mary's. "Sonia's a victim of abuse—her mother's and maybe others."

She stepped back, sat at her desk, raised a folder from her desk top. "Do you know what this is? This is Sonia's personal record, Mr. Lorenz. I cannot show it to you, but I can say that we had *reason* enough to withdraw her from the school." She waited but I wasn't getting it, so she added, "A person in her condition just cannot attend St. Mary's."

"Her condition?" I shouted. "Her condition is that she's being punished for her mother's sins."

"Mr. Lorenz," biting off my name fiercely, she hissed, "The girl is pregnant! Don't you see?"

"How do you know that?" I challenged. How could she know?

"By a test, Mr. Lorenz, a simple test which I myself administered here in this office."

I staggered at the bluntness of this—at the knowledge and its source. "What right did you have..."

"Every right, Mr. Lorenz. I remind you that this is a private school and you have a job to do in it—at least for now."

And that was it. I went out into the dark hallway and stood with my back against the cold wall. I saw images of Sonia alone on a street somewhere, and then of Maria with our child. They flashed alternately, then together. What sign was this? I went out of the building and into my car. An old cigarette butt in the back ashtray, I lit it. It smelled and tasted like burnt rope. I smoked it alone in the car. When I was done I went back inside to teach out the day.

Now I sit here parked along Elmwood Park. My lame leg beneath me, out on the walkway the dirty pigeons. I keep writing this down hoping each word, each sentence, will lead me somewhere, to a place where I can stand.

DOING WHAT YOU CAN

I did it. I called Sonia Mendozza at home from a pay phone, only it was her mother who answered.
"Yeah?"
"Hello, may I speak to Sonia?"
"Who is this? Is this you, Roberto, cause I'm telling you, kid, if I see you, I'll *kill* you."
"No, Mrs. Mendozza, this is not Roberto. I'm one of Sonia's teachers."
"Is this you, Lorenz?"
"Yes. This is Marco Lorenz."
"Hey, I'm glad you called, man. I been wanting to tell you something—Go straight to hell. You hear? Go straight to hell. What you mean starting in with my Sonia? Huh? She's bawling all the time now... cause of you starting something up with her. You hear me?"
"Mrs. Mendozza, you don't understand."
"I understand plenty, Mister. It don't take an education to see what's going on. You been stirring her up, making her hate me and our life."
"No. That's not true."
"Bullshit, it is, man. You're digging up old shit, telling her she's abused and all. Listen, man, do you want to have social services all over my ass taking my kids away from me? Do you?"
"I don't want to make things worse for Sonia. Could I just talk to her, Mrs. Mendozza? It's not right to take her out of St. Mary's like that?"
"She's pregnant! Or didn't you hear? How's she going to go to a Catholic school carrying a child?"
"I don't know that answer. Really, I just want to know that Sonia is alright. Is she?"
"Of course she's alright. She's with me. I'm her god damned mother, not you. Who are you to her anyway— some young guy with a gimpy leg should be taking care of his own damned business."

This woman was really getting to me. She knew every button to push. "Listen," I said, "if you care so much for your daughter, then take her to a good doctor and get her some counseling. She's a smart kid with a real gift for writing."
"Is that what this is about, her writing stuff?"
"No. It's about her welfare."
"Yeah, I hear you. But it's none of your damn business what I do with Sonia. She's my kid and not yours."
I could hear a Mendozza baby crying in the background. A radio was playing rap music. "Take care of her, please, Mrs. Mendozza. She's your gift of life." And I hung up. It was 3:30, and I had yet to drive home in the afternoon light of this late November day. It all felt like watching a ball roll down a hill in front of you, and knowing in your gut you could never run fast enough to catch up with it.

When I tell Maria the story of the phone call, she gets a little red in the face then sits down on the couch. I hang up my coat. She is breathing slowly like we practice for the natural childbirth. It is helping her take everything in. I sit down beside her.
"Oh, Marco," she says. "What did you expect from that woman? It's wrong as wrong, but some things you can't fix right away. Some things you just have to wait or accept."
"Are you saying I should stay out of it?"
"No, Honey, I'm not saying that. What I'm saying is some things you can't change and you can't let them hurt you so much. You have to know the difference between what you can change and what you cannot."
"You're sounding like a Twelve Steps program," I shoot back at her, but she pulls me closer on the couch.
"Today for example. I was sitting at the kitchen table ironing your shirts, but really I was worrying like I do. You know, how are we going to pay for everything when this baby comes? What if the baby comes early? What if something goes wrong and the baby is not okay, even not born at all? I can't help it, I thought it. And I kept ironing and a feeling came to me that whatever it is, we'll deal with it. Marco, I got myself to a place where anything is okay. It's

like we're all afraid of being dropped and the world it just goes on holding us up. Whatever little things tangle or come apart, something still holds us together."

She has this deep secret look in her eyes, and I lean over to kiss her forehead. "I hear you."

"And then, Marco, I got so quiet feeling the iron moving back and forth across the cloth, by itself it seemed, making everything warm and smooth. And I could feel the silence around me with no need to touch it. Do you understand?"

"I think I do."

"So, Marco, what I feel is going on is that there's something about this Sonia that connects to you. You can feel it too, I know. Maybe your mom and sister get mixed in there too. What do you think?" I say nothing, but look up into her face.

She says, "Oh, Honey, I don't have answers, but I feel inside that whatever it is you're to do, you'll do it when it comes time."

We both just hang there for a while in this silence. Outside you could hear a few cars passing the house. We both listen to it as the evening dark comes on.

Then Maria gets up and starts making a fresh pot of coffee. I put my bag of papers away on my closet work desk, and when I come back into the kitchen, a cup of coffee sits steaming on the table. For dinner we have a beans and pasta dish with fresh bread Maria has bought at Avanti's Bakery.

I am cleaning up the dishes, hustling them over to the sink when I hear Maria's laughter.

"What's so funny?" I ask.

"A story you made me think of."

"Tell it," I beg, setting down the last dish.

"Okay. This was a long time ago when I was in fifth grade. I was going to St. Mary's then and this Sister Aquinata was our principal. Did you ever hear of her?"

"No. You know I was a 'Public,' not a 'Catholic.'"

"No, I mean now. Do they ever speak of her at St. Mary's?" I shrug. "No, huh! Well they should, believe me.

That woman was a saint. Anyway, there was me and Loretta Gambino and Mary Alice Ferroni—I used to hang out with the Italians even then. Well, I snitched two packs of my mom's Winstons the night before, and so we met in the school parking lot and decided not to go into school that day. We decided to walk down to the lake instead, down to Lakeview Park where we would smoke our Winstons."

"You played hookie to smoke in the fifth grade!"

"Just wait. We lay down there behind a big log that had washed ashore. And we smoked them one after another—smoke after smoke, talking about boys and sex and stuff all morning. We'd take a drag and blow smoke up into the blue sky where the seagulls were circling around. And one of us would be telling a story or talking about someone. Later we walked along the beach poking things washed up in the sand. I don't know where the time went. You could say it went 'up in smoke' I guess, so that when 2 o'clock came around we were smoked out and headed back to school. See, we needed to sneak back onto the bus."

"You were a regular hoodlum then. My wife—I can't believe it."

"Well, as you could expect, we got caught. Sister Aquinata herself out of her office window saw us sneaking onto the bus. We were three happy girls laughing in our seats thinking we were home free, when her gray head peeks onto the bus. Then the rest of her is coming down the aisle like a locomotive. 'Off,' she says. 'You three girls. Off this bus right now.' She didn't have to raise her voice, cause we got up like puppets and danced out the door. 'Up to my office,' she says again as we come off the steps."

"You know, Maria, you probably have a record," I interrupt again. "I should check your permanent record to see what else you got into at St. Mary's."

Maria just stares at me. "Hey, you want to hear this?" I nod. "Well, then sister Aquinata did something wonderful see. Sure she told us about what a wrong thing we'd done, but she didn't hit us and didn't really yell. She didn't need to. She just looked into our faces and said, 'Girls, this school will punish you for breaking our rules, but for smoking the cigarettes — well, I'll leave that to *somebody* else. Now I know you three are sorry, so I'm going to let each of you tell your parents.'"

"God, how Catholic!" I exclaim. "Did you tell them?"

"Shhh," Maria scolds, "You're making this hard. Of course we told them. And I'll tell you something else. I sweated right through my blouse onto my jumper on the long walk home, and it was already October. We all got canned for a month, went to confession that night and every Saturday for a year. When I told my mom, she cried; then she made me go out to the garage and tell my dad. I remember he didn't say anything for a while; he was working on some carburetor. 'Come over here,' he said, and I was shaking. I remember he asked me what brand we were smoking; then he just lit up a Marlboro, and took a long drag. Without any words, he blew the smoke slowly through his white handkerchief. 'Look at this.' he said, and I did. This was some kind of magic. There was a bad stain there like you'd done something in your underwear. 'Maria, this is what you are doing to your lungs,' he said and thumped me with his forefinger on my chest. I was grossed out and, believe me, I got his message. I didn't smoke again for three weeks. I remember as I walked away, he finished his cigarette."

"That's a cool story, Maria. Can I steal it?"

"You haven't heard the coolest part. See, this Sister Aquinata, she knew what she could do and what she should not — what we had to do to ourselves. Am I making sense?"

"Yeah, I can see how it worked."

"Well, last year when my sister's girl Angela got in trouble for the same thing, I sat in my mom's kitchen remembering this whole time with her. I said how Sister Aquinata must have been a saint to know to trust us so hard. And Marco, I look over and my mother is either laughing or crying, cause her head is shaking so. She's laughing see, and she turns to face me. 'What?' I say hard. 'What is it?' And smiling back my mom holds my hand and says,

'Oh, Honey, Sister Aquinata called us and the other parents before you girls were out the school doors. She was taking no chances, believe me.' 'Damn,' I said shaking my hair, 'Damn,' and then it hit me—that old nun had something more to teach me. She was still giving me lessons, fifteen years later. Marco, she knew what she was doing, Sister Aquinata. She knew."

"Yeah," I say, "She was a saint of coolness." And I mean it.

MOLDING THE SHAPE OF THINGS

Today I come home from work and find that Margaret has stolen my parking space in the driveway. I park the Fairlane out on the street. A light snow just covers the grass. As I walk through it, I leave clear tracks in the white. Climbing these damn outside stairs I think to myself for the thousandth time how this is not a good location for a guy with a knee disability. But it has become our place and worth the hassle.

The house is so quiet—I wonder if Maria and Margaret are still here. Then from the bedroom comes the soft music of our "Deep Forest" CD. The sweet scent of a smoking incense floats into the living room—Margaret is definitely here.

"Hello," I call.

"Hello, Hon, we're in here," Maria calls back.

As I start to go in, I am suddenly stopped by Margaret's face, with its pointed nose and wide mouth.

"Wait," she says holding her hand up like a cop stopping traffic. "We're doing something in here. Let me explain it to you." But I push my way past her at the threshold. We're in my house now. And there in the light of the window curtains, sitting on a cushion on the dresser is my wife—completely nude and smiling back at me like a Buddha. On her huge chest and rounded stomach is a thick white gauze film the color of skimmed milk.

"Enter," Maria says barely moving her head. Her thick black hair is pulled back. I step forward into her smile, realizing I have never seen so much of this woman, never felt so strongly the bold fullness of her pregnant body.

Margaret brushes past me, reaches into a large metal bowl for another sheet of plaster gauze. I know the stuff well from the countless casts on my leg. They are making a legend, a body cast of Maria with child.

"I have to keep working on this," Margaret explains. "Before it dries." And I watch as she holds up the long strip, lets it drip softly into the bowl below.

"Isn't that going to be hot?" I ask.

"No, Dr. Marco, they're not hot anymore—it's a new kind of plaster they use."

"Oh," I say, moving closer to touch this living body shield. Maria is so huge, so rounded, her breasts and stomach so whole in the light. "Will it hurt the baby?" I ask. "Doesn't it scratch you?"

"No. I would never hurt this baby. And look, I'm coated with Vaseline." I see around the sides of her body a moist trail of Vaseline gel. I reach toward it.

"Don't touch, Hon. Not yet."

So I stand back looking at the figure of this earth mother goddess that I love. And then Margaret places her gauze sheet at the top of Maria's stomach just below her full breasts. Tenderly she strokes it with her hands, smoothing it over the crest of her dome. This is a woman to woman moment I am watching. Maria's face is Mona Lisa and Madonna, allowing the stroking to soothe her, to confirm her ample form—mother with child. Again Margaret's wet hands spread a layer of moisture over the entire dome of Maria's front. Both women smile quietly as the strokes move in a rhythm with and beyond the soft music and incense. I sit in the corner and I watch this rite so deep and real. And for the first time I am not jealous of Margaret. This time I quietly share her love for this woman Maria.

I wait and I watch as Maria smiles above the full globe of her body. I am one with them. When the music stops, I rise and go to make us all tea.

STANDING THE LINE

It's Saturday, the middle of November, and Maria and Margaret are going to Midway Mall to shop for baby things. When Maria holds up those little baby sleepers, her smile turns into tears of happiness. She strokes them softly and presses them to her cheeks. She's up about 40 pounds to around 165, which is pretty good for a small Chicano girl like her. I can image her waddling through the store, stopping at the Food Court to eat a fruit salad, and that Margaret's mouth will be going a 1,000 miles an hour.

For myself, I have something else in mind. Ted called last evening and asked if I could come out to support the picket line down in Oberlin. "Hey, Bro, I hate to ask it, but their UAW unit went into negotiations with management today. Most of their members will be in Michigan, so we're supporting their line. We sure could use some bodies to help us fill in."

I thought about it a few seconds — all the papers I have to grade, all that Ted and Marge have done for me, what the union means to these folks — "Hell, yes," I said, "Give me some directions."

I got up with Maria at about 7:00 o'clock and drank a couple cups of coffee while reading the paper and watching the "Today Show." It's stupid, but watching it is better than staring at Maria like I'm waiting for the baby to pop out. We ate the fresh oat bagels we bought at Baba's Bagelshop. About 7:30 I started dressing warm. Long underwear, undershirt and jeans, overshirt, sweater, thermal socks and boots. It's still November I can't forget, and there's not much warmth on a picket line. I threw on my Goodwill leather jacket and my cap, kissed Maria and headed out the door, down the long wooden stairs.

I'm sitting here now finishing my coffee in the car. It's a quarter to nine, when I should go on. The plant is called Thompsons Controls, and it's down in Oberlin's industrial park. It's back off the main streets, and I drove past it twice. Wait, Ted is getting in the car.

"Hey,"

"Hey,"

"What's going on with Maria?"

"Not much. Waiting. That's about it. Any day now. What's the story here?"

Ted is wearing brown thermal coveralls and his United Auto Workers jacket, a shiny navy blue nylon with the UAW crest sewn in gold on the front and back. He is sucking on a steaming styrofoam cup of coffee from McDonalds. "Well, this plant got started here over a year ago when Ford got rid of its seat making division. You know the story, the big guys don't want to pay the $19 an hour wages or the benefits we've earned, so they contract out to a plant which they've helped create. This little baby makes the seats for the vans at our Lorain Ford plant."

"So, what do they pay these folks?"

"Oh, about $8.50 and shitty benefits. That's what they're asking for, a fairer wage and a decent health care package." He blows steam against the frosting window shield. You can hardly see the white clouds passing by.

"So, what's Ford been doing for seats this week. Don't they have an inventory?"

"That's where we've got them, little brother. They created their own trap. Their 'just in time' supply policy may cut wages, but a strike leaves them out of seats in no time. They've already started using the amusement park's lot in Sandusky to store their vans. That costs them about $500 a van. Someone at the Union Hall said, 'A million a day, it's costing Ford.'" Ted nudges me with his fist, "Hell, man, Ford is now seatless. Seatless and strapped. They have to put the pressure back on Thompsons to deal."

Outside the window two women in parkas walk up. They tap on the window. Ted gives them the thumbs up sign. They look like mothers, but their rosy cheeked faces seem determined and somehow beautiful in the wind. It's time to get out and join them.

Ted wraps his big arm around me, says softly, "Appreciate this," and we walk on. A guy comes toward us in a black pea-coat and dark slouch cap.

"Ted, my man. How's it hanging?"

"Jimmy, you're right outta the 1930's in that outfit."

"Don't I know it. I found these at the Goodwill and I said to myself, I said, 'Man, I have to have this coat'...for outings just like this one."

"Well," Ted says, slapping him along the shoulder, "It's darn right *intimidating*."

Jimmy tips his head toward the security guard getting out of a parked van. "I hope *those guys* appreciate it."

"I sure do," I say smiling.

"This is my little brother Marco who's come down to join us."

Jimmy stretches forth his rough hand, "Yeah, I remember you, Marco. I was at the KOBE Strike back in 1987 when you got hurt." He looks down at my cane and waits.

I don't pick up his lead, and he understands. We all turn around and walk toward the burn barrels. A circle of a dozen men and women stand talking around the flames. They are doing that kind of walking-to-keep-warm dance you do in the cold, first one leg a little hop, then the other, then you move around in a little circle. They don't even know they're doing it. They all greet Ted with Howdies and Hello's, some wave so long to us; they've been out here already for hours. "Gotta keep our number at nine," Ted explains, then he shouts out to those leaving, "One Day More—Just think of it like that. Someone asks you how long you'll stay out, tell em' 'We're out here one day more than them.'"

"That's the way to take it," says an older guy in a hunting cap pulled over his ears. He is small with a deep etched face and comes walking towards us.

"God, Willy, I didn't recognize you," says Ted, and the two men give each other a long embrace. "Come over here. I want you to meet my brother."

Willy extends his hand as they walk towards me, "Good to have you with us," he says, and I pump his hand. For years I've heard Ted talk of Willy. He's been a union organizer since the 1930's.

"Willy here's been at it for around 60 years, Marco. The man is *history*." The others look around and someone laughs.

"Well, hey, I'm not 'history' *yet*," Willy laughs. "I'm still here in the flesh, though my mind gets lost sometimes." People laugh again, and Ted's face flushes pink in morning light.

"You know what I mean."

"Willy is a living legend," shouts Jimmy, and they all nod their heads in agreement.

We stand in the cold blowing across the roadway. Fifty feet away are the security guards imported from Pennsylvania in dark uniforms seated in their brown van. It's a stand-off marked by pink cones and green and white picket signs. Eventually Willy and another older guy named Paul begin marching up to the line and turning a sharp about face. The guards get out, we all laugh and cheer. Ted shouts, "My Daddy always told me, 'If you can't have some fun with it, don't do it.'" Willy stops in his tracks and points behind us.

Suddenly a truck toots its horn. Three of our people with signs come out in the street as a roadblock. The truck moves up the drive. Everyone suddenly grows stiff and silent. "Let's go talk with him," says Willy, and they walk down the street to his cab.

"Hey, there. How's it going?" shouts the truck driver.

"There's a strike going on here, fellow. These workers are out walking the line cause they want decent benefits. We'd appreciate your respecting our picket."

The man is looking out about 200 yards to the plant. The security guards are out with their video camera aimed at us. The line is about 30 feet away. "Damn!" he says, "No one told me nothing about this." We read the tension in his tired face, "I ain't never crossed no picket lines, and I ain't starting now," he says, and we all cheer. He throws it into reverse and begins backing out the drive.

We go back to the barrels and begin our watch. Jimmy goes to his car to telephone in the story of the trucker.

The time passes. People tell stories and talk... "Didn't I drive with you somewhere? Was it the Wheeling-Pitt Strike down in Steubenville?" ... "What's the news from the radio, anyone hear anything?" ... "Listen, we was just down at the Union Hall and they said Ford was going to shut down on Monday. That's what they said." ... "Alright, Ford!" ... "Anyone want some coffee? I got fresh in my thermos." ... "Look at those goons over there running back and forth to their commander. Here they come with their video camera. They got nothing else to do."... "Out here at night I like carrying my big flashlight with all those batteries. It makes a good club." ... "In the daytime you can roll up a newspaper tight and tape it, carry it in your back pocket. It works great and it's legal." ... "Here come some office people driving out, going to lunch. You got to let them go by, but turn your backs as they do." ... "Yeah, we're from human services, but we're with the college workers' UAW now. Our problem is our caseloads, we get overworked till we can't do the job right. You have to fight to do a good job nowadays."... "What time is it, *10:30*? God, it feels like noon." ... "Anyone want something from Burger King...We're making a run."

Someone goes off into the woods to gather more wood. You stare into the flames. Pieces of burning wood fall off and are lifted back into the flames. When the sparks and smoke blow into your face, you turn around. Smoke and cold fill your nose. The clouds pass slowly overhead, and you begin to read things into them. A woman speaks.... "You know, I'm a baker at the college. My son's been out of work for a month, and last week he was going to apply here. I said to him, 'Ray, don't you know them folks is on strike?' 'Yeah?' he says. And I say, 'Huh-uh, Hon. That's my union. I'm picketing out there.' And he didn't apply...but it's hard, you know. He's young and he needs the job."

Eventually the wind blows in at your collar, you start to shake a little and can't get stopped. In pairs you go off to warm up in the cars, yet you want to get back out there, because what keeps you going more than the stories or the knowing what's right are the faces of these others, the quiet passion in their eyes, the courage of their bodies facing the cold.

      I look around at Ted's face in the circle. He looks like Dad come home cold from the mill. His arm is around Willy's short shoulder, and he looks back strong into my own face.

WATCHING THINGS RISE

I wake this morning ranting at my aching leg, broken wing that it is, fragment that anchors my body to myself. I peel off the sheets, stumble into the bright lights of the bathroom and, yes, I talk to it. I scold it as I pull it up over the tub edge and into my bath—white sacrifice to the mill strike of 1987. I no longer curse the cop whose reckless club busted my kneecap forever. Instead I curse what is close, this withered piece of bone and flesh. For ten years now I've been an invalid, a man whose chief mark to most people is his disability.

I'll tell you, at first it was a wound, and I grieved and mourned it; then it became a weapon I used against everything, a reason to fail and a cause to hate the others. I came close to destroying myself with the hatred. Now it's become a tool, my ticket to a community of outcasts, my passport to a world of walking wounded—all of us really. If you ever forget that it's there, people will remind you. They either look at you or they look away. It comes to the same thing. I know that I remind them of that emptiness they feel in their own heart, that place where something is always missing or misshapen. Right now though I'm cursing it as the echo it is, of what's gone wrong and what's no longer there.

Maria doesn't see it that way and never has. She tells me I'll let go of this feeling when I don't need it anymore. I don't know about that. She kisses my leg as it lies naked on the bed, tells me, "Look at it, Marco. Listen to it." When she does that, it becomes something else, something soft and warm, my blood still pulsing through it.

Only sometimes I can't see it that way. Sometimes all it says to me is illness, the broken part of life echoing back. I see it now in young Sonia's pain and her carrying the sickness inside her. I see it in my mother's life, her disability brought on from the way her parents berated and used her. It wasn't the poverty nor the hard labor she endured. It was the sick and broken vision of herself and the world they drilled into her. "You're no good and never will be," they said. And she translated that back to Ted and me as "You go on, do something with yourself. Be something more than me and your father. We was never nothing. But you can be for us something in the world." That was always her way. She never saw it, how we're all somehow wounded.

Mom wouldn't talk about herself much, and I couldn't ask. Just piece by piece little things would come out. She'd be talking about something she remembered and suddenly she'd shut up. She'd turn away and do something in the kitchen—empty the sink of dishes, wipe a wet cloth across the counter again. Once though she was making bread on the kitchen table, breaking eggs into the floury mound of it. "Your grandma could make bread, you know," she said. "We'd do nine or ten loaves at a time, let them rise and bake all afternoon. Dump them out onto towels and spread them on the table to cool. Sometimes we'd eat a whole loaf, her and me."

I liked watching Mom talk like this as she tumbled the dough into itself, her little fists pressed into balls of dough. "So Grandma Kelly taught you to make bread, huh?"

That's when she'd do it, she'd remember something bad and go quiet as a rock. But this time I wouldn't let go. "Tell me, Mom. Tell me what happened then. Please, I want to know." And this one time she turned around to face me. I could see the way her face was warming up, tears coming in the pockets of her eyes. And this time she spoke.

"Okay, I'll tell you. I was ten that year, and Mama had gone to the store. I was to take the bread from the oven at four o'clock. Five times she told me this, 'At four you take out the bread.' She said it again and again. I knew my job, and so I sat in the kitchen staring at the clock for twenty minutes. I didn't want to mess up. But then my dad came bursting in. He was drunk and had fallen on the front steps. He was growling and his head was bleeding bad all over his face. I got him into the bathroom where he passed out on the floor. I started wiping his face with a wet towel, see.

His face had dirt and little chips of paint all over it. I was scared the way a kid gets. I thought he could die. I thought he could die and then what would we do?"

Tears were coming now as Mom sat looking towards me but seeing him. "I got him cleaned up and then I smelled it—the burnt toast smell of it filled my nostrils. Smoke was coming from the oven doors. I ran and I got them out somehow, just as I heard the back door slam. It was Mama, and she screaming, 'You little bitch. You little stupid bitch.' She yelled at me hard. I remember it. 'You burned my bread. You burned my bread!' And I started to explain, 'Mommy, Papa got...' But she had grabbed me by my hair twisting my neck. And she, she..." Mom's face got steely hard like I'd never seen. "She smashed my head into the window casing and the glass went crack. I was so afraid, but it didn't break. I busted my lip on the sill. I shook a minute and looked up to see her coming at me with her fists. I closed my eyes and then...nothing. When I opened them I saw Papa had ahold of both her arms. He was wrestling her saying, 'Stop, woman. Stop.' And I escaped. I ran to my room. I couldn't lock the door, so I hid under the bed." Mom looked straight into my eyes, "I don't know why I'm telling you all this," she spoke through tears. "I hid and I waited there for hours, but she never came. Never. And we never talked about it again. All that week we ate the bad bread I had burned. We never talked about the good bread I had ruined again." Mom had a hard look in her eyes; then she just looked away.

See, I can tell now that Mom never learned how to use her wound as a tool, because it was so deep inside her and it kept bleeding all through her life. They're such mean and senseless wounds, all of them. And this morning looking down at my mangled leg I see Mom's scared and twisted face, I see Sonia's trembling hands and averted eyes, my sister JoAnn's shrunken body, I see the wounds of us all and, yes, today I curse the pain of it all.

WAKING TO IT

Lately, I go to class and I teach the same thing again and again. It's hard to stay focused, cause I'm thinking about Mom and Maria and little Sonia. I tell my students to get out their workbooks and do the exercises on subject-verb agreement. Then we go over them. It's become sleep walking. Only when someone asks me something new do I awaken. We all have days like these, only mine seem close together lately.

Today, it is Laura who asks, "Mr. Lorenz, why don't you put poems on the board anymore?"

I look around at the empty board. I didn't even know I'd forgotten. Somehow, since Sonia disappeared, I'd stopped caring about that.

"If I can speak, Mr. Lorenz, some of us would like to talk about poems and stories again. Are we ever going to do any more of that?"

It is like a temple bell that awakens you to the sounds around you. "Yes," I say. "We'll do more of that, sure. You go ahead and do this exercise because it's part of your proficiency test, and I'll get a poem up there for the end of the class."

They are all looking up and some of them smile, I swear it. While they write, I look through our reader. Nothing seems right. Then I find it in a book I'd been carrying in my backpack, a little poem by Kenneth Patchen for his dead sister. I write across the board:

IN MEMORY OF KATHLEEN

How pitiful is her sleep.
Now her clear breath is still.
There is nothing falling tonight,
Bird or man,
As dear as she;

>Nowhere that she should go
>Without me. None but my calling
>Nothing but the cold cry of the snow.
>How lonely does she seem.
>I, who have no heaven,
>Defenseless, without lands,
>Must try a dream
>Of the seven
>Lost stars and how they put their hands
>Upon her eyes that she might ever know
>Nothing worse than the cold cry of snow.

When they are done, we read it once and then again aloud. It takes a while to get the tone and feel of it. I tell them the story of Patchen's dead sister being struck by a car as she ran out of church. She'd been practicing for first communion. Then something makes me tell them about my mother's death, her being run down by a car on the sidewalk along Broadway. The quiet of the funeral passing faces in the wintry streets. When I ask Laura to read it a final time, she reads it softly and when she comes to the part about "the cold cry of snow," I see that her tears match my own. I have inflicted my grief upon them. "I'm sorry," I say. "It's too sad. Forgive me."

"No," she says, "It's so beautiful. It's what poetry is for."

I stand silent in the light as the bell rings for the changing of classes.

TURNING THE INSIDE OUT

I am thinking of the story I did not tell my students today. It's as significant as the ones I did. I have to tell it here, because the one person I have not written about in all of this is my little sister JoAnn.

She was born a slow child, 'retarded' you would say, a sweet faced child with thin hair and big brown eyes. Next to my mother she became the emotional center and light of our family life. I remember how she would laugh so easily. As a baby and a little child she would clap her hands when you came home, then rock back and forth on the floor or in her seat at the table. "Mar-co," she would call. "Marco, you're home!" And I would be glad that I was. She would do this for everyone—she was the first person you'd go to whether you were happy or blue, cause she would know and accept you for what you were—always. She needed the same from us.

On Christmas of 1981 JoAnn started getting sick. By the Epiphany on January 6, we knew it was leukemia. She was nine years old. Mom took it hard. She kept saying, "My little angel. My little angel," then went into her bedroom for two days and wouldn't come out. Dad told each of us, "Listen, Ted and Marco, JoAnn has a disease—it's called leukemia, and it's not good. You're mom and I are dealing with it." We watched Dad take food in to Mom on tv trays, and then on Monday, Mom was there in the morning getting us off to school again—Ted and me. JoAnn was in the hospital for a while.

In the sixth grade study hall I went to the library and looked up the word "leukemia." It said, "Leukemia—a disease, is a purposeless, continued growth of white blood cells." I didn't understand what "purposeless" meant then, but watching little JoAnn getting sicker and sicker, I soon learned. She had the chronic kind where you get sicker and weaker, then are okay for a while, then get sicker again. It makes no sense, that's for sure, and the growth of these white cells went on unchecked, till anemia developed.

I'd come home from school and there would be JoAnn lying in bed with her blanket all rumpled about her where she was kicking because of the pain. Her little pale legs would be sticking out. The face would be hers, but the eyes were the darkness of pain. You'd turn to go and she'd wake up to see you and call your name, "Mar-co. Mar-co. Come here. Read me a story."

I read her the best... *The Velveteen Rabbit*, all of *Winnie-the-Pooh*, the poems of Shel Silverstein. But our favorite book, and the one that would always put her to sleep was by Randall Jarrell called *Fly By Night*. It had these dreamlike drawing by Maurice Sendak that she loved to touch. I'll tell it to you.

The story is about a boy who goes into a woods by his house, and he meets an owl. The owl's story is a poem. That's the part JoAnn just loved. Her eyes would open wide as she'd look up at mine. See, the owlet has to leave the nest so his family can have a baby sister owlet. He does, but "The world outside is cold and hard and bare." He goes from tree to tree till he finds a dead owl in the snow, and there high above is the cry of a small owlet. He flies hard and he reaches her in the nest. Then gradually they fly homeward till that night they meet the mother flying through the moonlight. The last part goes:

> at last they flew
> Home to the nest. All night the mother would
> > appear
> And disappear, with good things; and the two
> would eat and eat and eat, and then they'd play.
> And when the mother came, the mother knew
> How tired they were. "Soon it will be day
> And time for every owl to be in his nest,"
> She said to them tenderly; and they
> Felt they were tired, and went to her to rest.
> She opened her wings, they nestled to her breast.

We both loved that story. I know for me it was a comfort, telling me that little JoAnn would get well and be herself again with us. But she didn't. She got worse. The doctors tried everything—blood transfusions, cortisone treatment, chemotherapy, finally a bone marrow transplant. Each time she'd come a little out of the shadow of what was killing her; each time she'd drift back into it darker than before.

The bone marrow transplant was from me. I'm still glad of that. That summer we went into the Cleveland Clinic for it. We had the same room so we could talk or rest quiet together. We had the operation, and I went home first. Weeks later JoAnn came home. She was walking and talking and being her old self. I hugged her and hugged her. She was quiet and then she laughed, "Mar-co, it's just me. I've come home to you."

We all started forgetting about the shadow and then it came back again, darker and with less purpose than before. Her own body was killing her. JoAnn died that winter of 1982. There was snow on the ground. I remember I ran home from school to tell her something, but when I came in I saw how her door was closed. The silence in that house told everything. Mom called me in to her. JoAnn was lying there, her eyes finally closed. Her little body still. Mom said, "She loved you, Honey. She'll go on loving you forever." I believed her, I did, but still I wanted to cry out JoAnn's name. I wanted to curse at God for this crazy game, tell him he'd got the wrong person, but I didn't. I just let Mom hold me for a long time as she softly cried.

I know I carry her inside me on dark days and sunny, a quiet thing that keeps me human. I never speak of it because I figure no one can understand. I never dared to write it before, never thought I could. But if I can ever say anything right, it would be how JoAnn is still this white bird that flies through my heart forever.

WITNESSING THREE WONDERS

I can't believe it—light out of darkness—Three good things happened today. Do good things come in threes? I'll save the best for last.

First off, I went to the mailbox and there was a letter accepting one of my poems for the *Cincinnati Poetry Review*. I can't tell you how many rejections I've seen. It's hard to count snowflakes blowing back in your face. But here it was, my first poem acceptance. I can't wait to tell Maria. She's my greatest fan and critic. Whatever I read to her, she responds with "Great," but then after I'm grinning all over the house, she'll add, "It's great, Marco, but..." and then comes the real comment to deal with. "It's great but...did you mean to make it sound so ugly?" "It's great but...I lost track of who was who." "It's great but...do you think a woman would really think like that?" The thing is, she's usually right. She sends me back to the keyboard to work it over again. But sometimes, it's just "Great," punctuated with "I love it."

That's what she said the first time I read her this one. It's called "Voices in the Student Lounge" but the editor wants me to change it to just "The Student Lounge." What it is is a simple record of some of the conversations I was hearing out at LCCC while I was sitting in the lounge waiting for classes to start. It's bits and pieces of the life going on, and I just listened. It was weird really, because I'm used to putting myself right in the middle of all that I write. It's always what's happening to me; only this time it was my hearing the lives of these others that was happening. So I just let it.

People ask me sometimes what the students are like at a community college. They ask you that as if you could tell them. I mean the students are all so different. I can't say anything in general that isn't a lie, a stereotype. It's a case where the more you know about it, the less you know to speak. I tell these people, "Come on out. I'll introduce you to some of them," but they never do. So what I found myself doing in this poem was just becoming this strong and steady listening. I know it's a little rough still, but here's a piece:

> A woman sits down heavy on the couch.
> Each of us let out a huff of air:
> "I got three kids at home you know
> waiting for me when I get out of here. Three kids
> asking me each morning, 'Mommy, when'll you
>   be home?'
> I tell them, I try to explain, and they listen
> but they don't understand. They ask instead, 'Do
>   you have
> to go to school? When is Daddy coming home?'
> That's when I want to tell them their father
> ain't coming back here no more cause he's
> sitting in a prison cell down in Mansfield
> looking out at birds and sky through bars.
> I want to tell them that, but I can't.
> I ain't got the heart."

The whole poem goes on like that, a string of voices from those trying college like it's their first or last chance they'll ever get. My writing teacher said it was an ethnography poem, and I nodded my head but I had to look it up. He's right, it's just a record of life from what's spoken there.

    Well, that was great, but when I opened the second letter, my heart started thumping. I have been writing this book about living in Lorain and the steel mill strike of 1987. It's based on my own life and 90% of it is true as true. *Beyond Rust* it's called, though I first thought of calling it "Sweet Lorain" like the song. Somebody said I should call it "Sweat, Lorain," but I figured they were joking. Then I watched this television special with Ted and Marge and their kids called "Life in the Rust Belt." It's a documentary done right here in Lorain. I liked the show but hated the name..."the rust belt." What a crock—to define a place by its worst element. I said, we should call the corn belt the Cow Shit Belt, and New York could be the Crack Belt, but that just brought a laugh. Nobody seems to feel it as much as I do, that we're more than our rust. Hell, rust is a steel worker's nightmare. So I say we're living on and "after" the rust of this economic decline; "beyond" the rust to where our real lives go on. I feel it everyday when I'm out at the college or when I'm teaching my eighth graders. We do get by somehow. I wanted to write of that.

I almost forgot, the good thing was that this publisher that Dr. Franco told me to send my book to, well, they really liked it. They're not sure yet, but their editors are all reading it. It's a small Midwest outfit, so I won't make any money on it, but that was never what that book was about. Wonder of wonders, by next year I could have a little novel published. It's too unreal to describe.

But that's not even the best news, though it's getting impossible to rank them. The best news is that Maria has taken Sonia Mendozza to see Sylvia, a social worker at the Sharing Tree. Maria, that pregnant woman who listens and knows, she just stepped in and broke the paralysis we all were stuck in. She just did it.

Yesterday was Saturday and I was at home watching the American Movie Classics channel. *Lonely Are the Brave* was on, with Kirk Douglas as this beat up modern cowboy who can't let go of the range life. It's great. Anyway, I'm watching it and feeling good and sorry for my life and all when Maria says she is going to the store. I say, "Wait, I'll go with you...after this movie." But she already has her coat on and in a moment is gone. I hear her drive away and then get back into my movie. About 50 minutes later when the movie is over, I realize she hasn't returned. I get up and look out the window. That never does any good, but we all do it, right? Then I think maybe I should call someone, but who, Rini-Rego Market? "Hey, I'm looking for a very pregnant woman in a green coat." Actually that might have worked. I could call the hospital but don't. What I do is I call Esther, but Maria isn't there, so I sit at the table and I wait. I make a pot of decaf and I wait. Nothing. Where is she?

And then she comes in. "Hi, Hon, sorry I'm late," she says shaking the snow off of her boots.

I don't speak. I just wait for the excuse.

"Promise you won't get mad?" she asks. "Promise, and I'll tell you something good."

"Why should I get mad if it's good?"

"Cause, I did something without asking you, that's why. I did something I had to, Marco. Please understand. I went to Sonia Mendozza's house."

"You did!"

"Yeah, I got so sick in my heart thinking about her. I knew you were stuck, and I thought, why am I waiting for Marco to figure this out? I'm a woman, I can handle that mother of hers. I owe it to that girl like she's a cousin of mine, or a sister. I don't know. I just knew I had to do something."

"God, what happened?"

She is taking off her coat now and hanging up her scarf. "If you can wait, I'll tell you everything, but first, I have to pee." She disappears into the bathroom and I fix us both a cup of decaf. She comes back and sits down. I help her off with her boots. Her cheeks are still pink and a little damp.

"At first, Marco, she wouldn't let me in. She cursed at me on the porch like a witch. I didn't care, after what she has done to little Sonia, I had to do something to reach her. So, I start talking to this woman like a friend. 'Okay, now, Mrs. Mendozza, I come here to help you, like a friend.' I opened my coat to show her my big belly. 'Look at me, I'm almost a mother, like you. Please, let me in, I have to *pee*.' And she did it. Pretty soon I was inside that house apartment sitting on the couch. Sonia and her little sister peeked their heads around the corner at me. I knew I had to make good, so I started asking her how she liked living in South Lorain. She lives about 5 blocks from us, you know?."

"And this wild woman talked with you. I can't believe it."

"Yeah, she did. She told me where her people were from, how many of them lived in Lorain County, what a slob her husband had been deserting her and her four kids. I told her, 'I know, men are all pretty much worthless.'"

"Thanks, for sacrificing us, really."

"Well, it was worth it, you know. She opened up a little, and then she said it, 'I tell you, I don't know what to do.' And I waited a little and then I said, 'How about you let me help you? Even though I'm big and pregnant, I know what you're saying. You have nothing to be afraid of. I'll just help you by helping Sonia.' She looked up at me like a starving person. 'Alright,' she whispered, 'You can talk to her. Sonia, come in here.' And Sonia was right there. She'd been standing around the corner listening. 'Hi, I'm Mr. Lorenz's wife. We live just a few blocks away.' She nodded and sat down on a straight chair. Like you said, she won't always look you in the eye, but anyway I said, how about going with me to get some groceries? You could help if you'd like. And the mother nodded and Sonia got up and got her coat. Only we didn't go to the grocery store, we went over to the new coffee shop where we met with my friend Sylvia."

"Sylvia, how did she get into this?"

"I called her before I went to the Mendozza's. I told her most of the story and asked if she could just talk with the girl. She was there in the coffeeshop waiting for us. It was a good scene. Everyone got to know each other. When Sonia walked back to the house with me, she gave me her hand. And, if this big baby doesn't come bursting into the world before the end of the month, I'm going to meet Sonia each Wednesday for a while."

"God, Maria, you're wonderful." I was really so happy. I don't know why. It felt so good and right.

"You see, Marco, we women have a thing. Sometimes we get pushed into a hole, but then we can open like flowers. It's how we get along."

All I could do was nod, again and again.

So Maria and Sonia are the third wonder and the greatest. Three in one day. I think I'll just go to sleep before anything can go wrong.

LAYING PEOPLE OFF

Marge called this morning before either of us were really awake. I was trying to get my own voice working when I heard the alarm in hers.

"Marco. It's Ted. He's gone. He went out to the Union Hall yesterday and hasn't been home since. Marco, I'm scared."

I was suddenly awake, but I couldn't figure it. "Did you call the Union Hall? What's been going on?"

"Yes, five times I called them. They say nothing is going on. The meeting was about the lay-offs."

"What lay-offs?"

"Marco, where have you been? Ford is shutting down two lines — the Thunderbird and the Cougar. They're about to lay off 2,000 men and women."

"Jesus, Mary, and Joseph! That's brutal. How'll it affect you and Ted?"

"Oh, God, you know how he takes every lay-off personal. This time it is. This time, Marco, it's Ted's job that's been cut out from under him. He's one who'll go after 10 years. He's got 10 years at the mill, 10 at Ford...he's one of the expendable ones."

"I'm sorry, Margie. I didn't know." I felt like such a dope, "We've just been caught up in the baby and all."

"We didn't say nothing cause it wasn't for sure until last week. Ted told me, 'Don't bother them. Their plate is full.' And I wouldn't, Hon, only I'm desperate to know what Ted's gone and done."

For a moment we could each hear ourselves breathing on the phone...the silence of ignorance and pain, of thinking it through from inside of Ted's heart and brain.

"French Creek," I said.

"What?"

"I think I've got it figured...If he's not with the union, he might go out there. I'll dress and drive out, and I'll call you soon as I know anything. Okay?"

"Oh, God, Marco. He's been so desperate this week. It's like I don't know him. I'm so scared."

"Hold on Margie. Do you want me to bring Maria out there with you?"

"No, don't bother a sleeping mother. I'll be okay. I was going to start calling around to see if I could get some houses to clean. Only I can't till I hear about Ted. Call me right away. Okay?"

Throwing on my jeans and jacket, I stopped to run a wash rag across my face. Looking in the mirror I tried to see Ted's face in my own. "What's up?" I was asking aloud as Maria came in.

"Honey, what's going on?" she asked, making her way to the toilet. She lifted her soft gown and sat like a sleepy queen. *What to say?* I told her.

"Ted's been gone all night—I'm headed over to French Creek Park to see if he's there."

She rubbed her eyes and face, looked up helplessly, "Why?"

"Ford," I said. "They're laying him and 2000 others off, probably for good. Shutting down two lines. When they shut them down, they never open them up again."

"Those bastards," Maria said, wiping herself. "They're going to kill this town."

"Ford," I said again like it was a person, like it meant anything. It was just a force, a machine—the company, the corporation, the institution that we all live with, that can affect all of our lives.

There was that silence again, and then Maria flushed and I went out the door. I was tying my shoes when she stroked my hair. "You're doing what's right, Honey. You can't take it all on, just help your brother right now."

I kissed her and went out the door.

Here I am driving down East River Road to the place where it all happened—the steel strike of 1987 where I lost my knee joint in an instant...the whack of a club wielded in fear and rage. There to the left is the back of USS/KOBE Steel, those mills that fed us and ate our fathers' lives.

At Colorado Avenue I stop and park the car, walk out through tall wet grass into the morning mist. I walk a long ways, till I come to the creek, push the bushes back with my cane, and there on the big rock is Ted, sitting on a tarp with a blanket wrapped around his big shoulders. He looks small somehow as he turns to see me.

"Hey, bro," he says. "I been waiting for you."

"Hey, bro," I say back, bending to sit beside him. "I'm here."

We talk softly as the birds sing around us. And there is the sound of the creek and the Black River, each of them flowing near us. He tells me he drove his new Ford van out to the Ford Credit Office where he left it blocking the driveway. "Let them figure out what to do with it. I don't want it." He had walked half way back to town when he got a ride to Sheffield, then walked out here to where he and Dad and I used to come to fish.

"Ted," I say, folding my arm around him there on the rock, "Ted, it isn't you. It isn't you that's wrong. It's the same damn betrayal that happened to Dad."

We both sit silent, feeling the morning around us, the soft call of mourning doves. Then he says, "I know that now. I just got confused, caught up in the current," and he throws a single stone into the water. We watch it disappear. Then I throw another beside his. Again we watch. Then he throws a whole handful and so do I, both of us laughing as we rise.

In the end, each of us knows what matters, that Ted and Marge, Maria and I, are more real than all of our problems. Turning onto East River Road, I look over at my brother and know again how life isn't about seeing through people but about seeing people through. We drive home to Marge and Maria.

LEARNING BY GOING

Maria has been walking up and down the hallway all afternoon. Her soft slippered footsteps have become a kind of music while I work. I am lying across the bed grading the papers of my classes, essays on the theme of lessons learned from life. "Tell a story of an experience in which you learned something about life." Okay, many of them are simple, lessons from one of the Ten Commandments. They must be going over that in religion class. Still, they are describing their experience and that's what counts. Another bunch are about learning something about friendship — trusting and caring. A few deal with families, working with parents, accepting a new child as sister or brother. I like grading them.

Maria brings a fresh cup of coffee into the room, sets it on the corner of my desk. I look up as she sits down on the desk chair. She has on a pale blue dress with a black sweater. Her face is like a map, so many lines but I don't know which state we're in. She lets out a little puff of air, not really a sigh, a kind of release valve.

"Oh, Marco, I'm scared." Her expression hangs in space. I lay my papers down upon the bed.

"Scared?"

"Yes, about the baby, the hospital, you know, the thought that things could go wrong. Last night I dreamed my father. He was dying in the hospital and when I bent over him his face was that of a child." Maria always takes her dreams as portents she interprets to me. "I think he was the baby — our unborn child."

"Yeah," I nod, thinking this one through. "Probably."

"He was in a hospital dying and he was a child being born. Don't you see?" She was pressing my hand now with her own trembling one.

"Well, Honey, your father did die in a hospital," I say, but she shakes her head.

"Yes, and what about the baby, Marco?" She is shaking as she says it. "Is she to go with him?"

I feel the weight of this thought go through my body. It's a strange and fearful sadness like I'd entered a dark river. We'd been walking along the edge of this for months, afraid to cause a wrong by thinking or saying it. Now we are into it, with the cold waters rushing around us.

"Was the baby alive in your dream?"

She thinks about it. "I try hard to remember. I can just see her face and that's when I awaken. It seemed that she was. Yes, there was a kind of helpless look on her face like she wanted something of me...but I couldn't tell what, I couldn't understand and I couldn't help. I was paralyzed by a pain in my body." Maria begins crying softly, and I move over to hold her.

"It's okay, Maria. These are real fears. You're allowed to have them. They're natural. I have them too. But that doesn't mean they're going to happen."

She looks up at me and back down. "There's something else. I didn't want to tell you...Margaret and I, we were doing the Ouiji board at her place yesterday, and when we asked it for the baby's sex, it wouldn't move. It wouldn't go, it just stayed in one place. It scared both of us, so we quit."

"Ah, the Ouiji. Didn't we agree to not do that anymore?"

"We were just playing," Maria says like a child now. "We tried that simple question just to see what it would say. We didn't expect it not to answer."

"But it did, Maria. It told you, 'Don't ask,' that's all. It agreed with me."

We both smile at this, though I feel her still trembling. I kiss her sweet hair.

"Well, it's more than this," Maria says, serious again. "I didn't want to start anything, but I can feel the baby moving around like it wants to come out—today, right now. I mean it."

I sit up. "Have you felt any contractions?"

"I don't know. I think so. I've had a kind of cramping pain all afternoon."

"Why didn't you tell me?" I am standing now, beginning to pace around the little bedroom. "Should we call the doctor?" I ask.

"No, I don't think so. Nothing really has happened to say yes. I haven't lost my mucous, my water hasn't broken. These feel like cramps, not like labor pains." Reaching my hand and placing it over her round stomach, I listen, "I just wanted to warn you," she sighs. "I couldn't keep it all inside."

And we both smile at her words, our eyes big and wide. "You may not have to," I say and sit back down beside her. We are gently rocking as tears well from our eyes.

"We'll take this step by step," I assure her. Then I ask, "What should we do next?"

At four o'clock we call Doctor Esposito at the health department. She says to wait till the contractions become regular. We know this, we've been taught this in the child birthing classes, but this isn't a class, it's suddenly a real birth we are dealing with.

"I don't think I should eat anything," Maria says, "But can I make you something?"

"No. No. I don't think I can eat. I'll get something if I can. I don't want anything...except this baby and relief. You know it feels like a fire is going on inside of me. Do you feel that?"

She gently nods. "It's like my body has been prepping for this for months. My body has its own mind — the baby's."

We are sitting on the couch now waiting. Maria picks up the remote and flicks on the set. Rosie O'Donnell is halfway through her show. She has Diane Keaton on, and they are talking about their babies. Maria looks up, "You know, I love Rosie, but she didn't have that kid...didn't swell up like a blimp and go through this river of pain I'm swimming in."

"I know."

"She's being a good mom, but..." Maria gasps for a second, "It's another pain...Umm. Marco," She gasps again. "Mark the time." but I have already written it down.

We had agreed to handle this ourselves, but around 5:30 we call Maria's mom. Esther asks all the right questions, says to call her when we head for the hospital. I envy the way she knows how to wait. Every time I look up it seems the clock is stuck or broken—hardly any time has passed and yet Maria is clearly moving forward, wading down and into the river of it all.

"Marco," Maria calls from the bedroom where she has gone to lie down.

"Another contraction, Maria?"

"No. I want to ask you something, about the baby's name. I want to see if we agree." I walk into the bedroom and Maria is sitting up. "If it's a boy..." she prompts.

"We call him Paul."

"Right. But if it's a girl...and it will be."

"What? What have we decided, Maria Concita Rosalita Gomez Lorenz?"

She smiles calmly, "I say, 'Rosa' for your mother Rose and my grandmama Rosalita."

It is the first time she has suggested it, and it sounds so right. I say it, "*Rosa*...Sounds good to me."

"It is, Marco. It's right. It will be Rosa." And for a moment I can see my mother holding the child, a child who would not hide in corners or be ashamed as she, a child of Maria who would be brave and strong and beautiful, a child of Maria and Marco Lorenz.

"Oh," Maria's eyes go up and down. I look at my watch.

"Oh, Maria," I say, "we are heading for the hospital."

LABORING

Maria as been sweating through the labor pains. I stand at her side, as she clutches my hand, and I coach. She puffs like a locomotive working through the pain. Then she sighs and looks up and I feel her swimming through miles to this. It's as though the pain wants to push her back, but she swims on right through the biggest waves. We've done this for three hours now in this little labor room, yellow walls and blue curtains. They and the furniture are the clothes of this birth.

Esther is driving in now that the labor pain is down to every three minutes. The nurse smiles and says, "Your wife is at 5 centimeters."

I smile back, "Is that good? I forget." It's like reading a map — how many miles before we're there is all you want to ask.

"Yes, I'd say that's good for now," she says.

"How much longer — do you think?"

"Oh, you'd have to ask the doctor, but it's too soon to tell. It could be an hour or as many as ten or more." I nod, and she touches my arm and nods back, "We can't know these things. Someone else is in charge."

I'm thinking God...but then I think Maria, no the baby. Yes, it has its own power — we both know that. Maria more than anyone...she's felt its every move going on. What I know comes from touch and from listening to Maria talk, seeing the way she's grown. Maria knows from inside.

It is two a.m. and Maria seems to have gone out of labor — Is that possible? It's an intermission, and somehow she's been able to sleep. The nurse and Esther tell me to sleep too, but I just can't. I write in this. If I could crawl in next to Maria, I know then I might sleep, but she might wake into a pain that would kick me out. I stand at her side, at the railing, and watch her breathe. She is so beautiful —

her black hair in wet ringlets matted against her soft face. I'm afraid to touch her, so I count her breaths, make them my own.

Three a.m. and the labor pains have begun again, only harder this time. "Oh, God—Oh, God—Oh, God!" Maria calls out in the middle of each. "Help me," she cries out, and I'm so damned helpless. The pain in her voice cuts through me like glass. "Mother Mary..." she cries out and comes through to the end. She is seven centimeters and the doctor smiles up at me.

"We're nearing the birth, Marco. It will be coming soon."

After she says this, nothing happens for a long time—another hour with no real pains. "I don't know how she does it, Marco," Esther whispers."Look, that girl has fallen back to sleep. She always did that as a child. She would be sick or have cramps real bad and just disappear. I'd find her in bed, sound asleep, all curled up like a flower."

For some reason I begin to cry, just softly the tears come up out of my throat and into my eyes. Esther comes over and holds me, the two of us hovering around Maria and this unborn child. "How is Luis doing?" I ask. He's been struggling through a gall bladder operation.

"He's doing okay, Marco. He'd be here with you if he could. You know that." She's right, I do.

At 4:30 the doctor says, "Maria and Marco, I'm going to try something to help bring this baby along. Listen now. Everything is fine, but I know you're exhausted, and if it delays too much longer we might have to take it...by Cesarean. So I'm going to see if I can help stretch your membrane—to break your water sack. Is that okay with you."

"Is that normal?" Maria asks.

"It's normal in a case like this," the doctor says.

We look at each other and Maria says, "Yes, let's do it. Let's help our baby come to us." I nod and the doctor slides under the sheet, reaching up into the body of this birth.

In five minutes the water breaks and the labor takes over again with new force. Maria's eyes are wide and she forgets the breath—she just bears down and grunts through pain into the push of it. I hold her arm, and she pulls away. "No...not now...don't touch..." I let go and watch.

Esther whispers, "It's okay, I remember doing that. It's so much her pain, she needs all herself to face it."

They're a minute apart and the doctor is telling her to "Push, Maria...push harder ... harder..."

"I can't do it," Maria shouts... "I can't do it," and her breath goes out.

"You're doing fine, just fine," the nurse says wiping Maria's brow. I can't move, but a part of me wants to fly...it hurts so to see her in such pain. We men are so helpless and cowards.

"This is it, Maria. The head is crowning. Push hard with all of your might." And she does — the muscles and breath are in a great rhythm of strength — she screams out — "Uhhh! Mother Mary, Uhhh!" The doctor is moving the baby's head out and into the light; it's so red and wet and alive and just sliding along. The shoulders are coming next...

"Wait.." the doctor cries out...I can see her hand reaching down the baby's back, "Okay, Push — Push — Push," she calls, and Maria does it like it's one long wave she is pushing our baby along — Out it comes.

"Maria!" I shout. "She's out!" And Maria's head is thrown back. "It's a girl, Maria. It's our Rosa." Isn't this the time they lay the baby on the mother's breast? But the doctor is holding her. I can't see. Silently she is cutting the cord, a thick fibrous thing.

"It's okay," says the doctor, but there is a new strain in her voice. "Nurse, come around here." They take the baby over to a table, while the other nurse is cleaning up Maria. No stitches — just the blood and placenta to be cleared and taken away. Esther and I each hold Maria's hands. She is trying to look down at her baby, but all we see are the white and pink backs of the doctor and nurses. They are turned from us, working on baby Rosa.

There comes the baby's cry and with it a deep ripple of joy and tears. The sounds of her are so sweet it brings laughter and tears together. They turn and we see they have wrapped her in a tiny white blanket. Doctor Esposito is carrying her over to us. "My God how beautiful!" Esther calls out.

"She is beautiful and breathing fine," the doctor smiles, laying her on Maria's breast. Maria's face is a Madonna of light as she kisses this little face so fresh from her womb. The flower of Rosa is soft in Maria's arms, and for a moment I see in Rosa's face the face of Maria and Esther. I see the faces of my lost mother and sister. I let go and see all that I am. Maria reaches up for me, and I bend to kiss baby Rosa whose touch is tender and light yet full of the weight of what is real. There is this moment that will live forever.

Then the doctor's words, "Maria and Marco, there is something I need to tell you. Your baby is healthy, but there is a slight deformity. I need to show you," and she begins unwrapping the blanket. No one is breathing as the blanket unfolds and we see it—the hand, the left hand, it is tiny and unformed...there are no fingers, only a thumb and a blob—a mitten hand. We all breathe in and hold... "The cord was wrapped tight around her forearm and the blood couldn't get through—so the hand couldn't develop. The other is fine. Look," and she shows us the unfolding hand with each tiny finger. But this only makes the other more grotesque. No one is speaking, and then Maria starts crying hard, loud sobs coming out of her throat.

"Oh, my God. What have I done? What did I do to our baby?" I hold fast to her arm, but she turns away.

"No, Maria. It's not you." The words come boiling out of me, "It's God who's done this to us." We are both so torn by love and pain—the call to care again deeper, the denial of relief — we cry together in the swirling center of it. A silence holds us all. The last thing I remember is Esther holding our Rosa in her arms gently swaying back and forth and humming softly in the bright light of that huge room.

DELIVERING

Two long weeks have passed and I didn't have the heart to write in this journal.

The first week was quiet except for Esther, who moved in with us to help Maria and, of course, the baby, whose sounds fill this so empty house. I guess I am the one most quiet, because I do hear Maria talking at times with Esther and Margaret, but not with me. If I'm in the bedroom, I close the door, yet through the wood I hear the sound of crying, the fresh raging of tears, the soft hum of comforting. I hear it but I can't taste it. Maria says such fierce things. Yesterday it was, "My sins brought me this. I broke my baby's life." I don't know what to say to that except, "No, you've got it wrong, Maria. It's God's mistake, not ours." She just turns away, goes into her bedroom and cries softly alone. I sit on this couch and try to watch tv.

This morning I was sitting at the table trying to eat some dry toast with my coffee and Maria was at the sink with her back to me. "Don't hate God, Marco." she pleaded, "Hate me, please!" I got up and went over to her, but she ran away into the bathroom. I tried to catch her and bumped my knee on the coffee table. "I love you, Maria," I cried at the door. "I do." Nothing.

When I hold Rosa, I try not to look at the hand, but when I do, I see all the wounds I've known—my own broken limb, my mother's being killed by a drunken driver, little lost JoAnn, the senseless pain of Sonia Mendozza, Maria's hurt and blame—all the scars of the world, the wounds of this abandoned town. Rosa is another, and yet hers is the one wound I can't bear. I turn hard as the stone of my parents' grave.

Mostly there is quiet here, and yet you hear everything. The setting down of cups, the placing of dishes on the sink, the sliding of chairs across the linoleum floor, the soft rush of cars outside, the sounds of sorrow inside. The television is so empty now. I can't watch and I can't read. I've forgotten how to laugh or to care.

Thursday night Esther was eating with us. "Maria and Marco, please listen," she said "You're in grief. You have lost something and it's natural to grieve." Maria and I looked at each other. We were listening with our hearts. "And please hear this with the love from which it comes. The something you've lost, the something you grieve—it was never there. You never had it, never, and so it isn't lost. Please, my children, love what is there."

I know what she said is true, but I don't want to hear it. It is I who always wraps Rosa tight with the blanket, keeping her arms closed inside. And it is Rosa who struggles to get them out. It is our perfect little Rosa that we are missing, and yet here she is in our lap. Is our loss real or not? I know all this but still can't act.

Another ten days of this empty sorrow, and Esther has moved back home with Luis. I am back to work. Because Maria still needs someone to help getting along, we have hired someone, Sonia Mendozza. She is here each day talking with Maria, reading, writing, changing the baby and cleaning. She's about four months pregnant now herself. Being here has been good for her I think. Not just the knowing what to expect, more the being a person whose help is needed and respected. Maria calls her, "My little sister Sonia," and they understand each other in ways we used to, Maria and I.

Today when I came home form work, I couldn't find them. Then I saw Maria sleeping peacefully in the bedroom. Sonia had left a note, "I'm taking Rosa out for a walk to the Park in her buggy. It's a warm January day and the streets are sunny. I figured what could it hurt."

It is Rosa's first walk. Maria and I hadn't even thought of taking her out. I take my after-school nap, and when I wake, Sonia is sitting across from me. Her cheeks are red from being outdoors. She lays Rosa beside me. "Here, you hold her while I bring up the buggy," she says and is gone.

I open the blanket and look at her, "Rosa," I say, "You are my rosebud." And it's true, her face and cheeks are as fine and radiant as a rose. I take off the outer blanket and begin unbuttoning her wrapper. Her hands go up to her face. She moves those arms about like a wild puppet, and then the tiny hand strikes her eye. She blinks hard and quick — What is this? She begins doing it again and I almost stop her when she does something new, she brings the tiny hand to her lips and begins to softly suck. She sucks and her eager eyes say yes, she is pleased with this. I laugh for the first time in weeks. And then Sonia is there at my shoulder watching.

"You have a beautiful child," she says. "Everyone loves Rosa. Everywhere we went, everyone loved her." And she scoops her up. "Time for a change," she says and disappears into the bathroom. I get up and put the kettle on for a cup of tea.

When Maria awakens, Sonia has already gone. I am sitting in the rocker given to us by the teachers at St. Mary's, and I am laughing with Rosa, rocking and holding her up close to my face. I don't even hear Maria till she puts her soft hands on my face, "Oh, Marco, I love you so much. I've been so lost without you." And we kiss again full and deep. I feel Maria falling into me and close my eyes. When I look up she is bringing Rosa's tiny face up close to ours — three faces touching in a ring of love.

Outside is the sound of traffic, the slow boom of the mills, the clash of a train starting up. And inside is a man and a woman and a child. The man holds the child's tiny hand up and presses it to his lips, kissing her wound again and again as his own.

(Author's daughter Laura, grandchild Rosa, and self, 1997)
© photo by Kat Neyberg

Larry Smith grew up in the industrial Ohio Valley in the 40's and 50's; his family were railroaders and riggers and homemakers. He worked for a time in the steel mills along side of his father. His education included a bachelor's degree from Muskingum College in 1965 and a master's and doctorate from Kent State University in 1974. He began his teaching career as a high school English teacher in Euclid, Ohio, and is now a professor of English and Humanities at Firelands College of Bowling Green State University in Huron, Ohio.

He is the author of six books of poetry, two literary biographies of Kenneth Patchen and Lawrence Ferlinghetti, and the novella *Beyond Rust* (Bottom Dog Press, 1995) set in industrial Lorain, Ohio, and featuring the main characters Marco and Maria.

He has read from his poetry and prose at conferences for writing and labor, including the North American Labor History Conference at Wayne State University and the Working Class Studies Conference at Youngstown State University. He is also an editor and publisher at Bottom Dog Press.

He and his wife Ann live in Huron, Ohio, near the town of Lorain where his fiction is set.

RIDGEWAY PRESS BOOKS
Since 1974

1990
The Violence of Potatoes,
  Faye Kicknosway
snakecrossing,
  Lolita Hernandez
Blood M. Ther,
  Lorene Erikson
Salad in August,
  Stella L. Crews
Conformities,
  Laurence W. Thomas

1991
Pierced by Sound,
  Lawrence Pike
Home Before Light,
  Cheri Fein
(US),
  Michael Castro
Bearing Witness,
  Bob Hicok
The Lingo of Beer,
  Rudy Baron
A Passionate Distance,
  Joan Gartland
Gittin Down:
An Anthology of Prison Writings
The Cursive World,
  Marc J. Sheenan
Deliver Me,
  M. L. Liebler
Labor Pains,
  Edited by Leon Chamberlain

1992
Stations of the Cross,
  John R. Reed
A Modern Fairy Tale: The Baba Yaga Poems,
  Linda Nemec Foster
Listen To Me,
  Faye Kicknosway
The Vision of Words: Michigan Poets,
  Edited by M. L. Liebler
  Photographs by John Sobczak
Hacking It,
  Jim Daniels
On A Good Day,
  Gay Rubin
de KANSAS a CALIFAS & back to CHICAGO,
  Carlos Cortez
Mystical,
  Dalmation
Deer Crossing/Leap Years Away,
  William Boyer
Fragile Visions,
  Josef Bastian
Raking the Gravel & Other Poems,
  Ben Bohnhorst
Macro-Harmonic Music Manuscript Workbook,
  Faruq Z. Bey

1993
Hunger And Other Poems,
  Geoffrey Jacques
Mysterious Coleslaw,
  Pamela Miller
Still Life With Conversation,
  Rebecca Emlinger Roberts
The Short Life of The 5 Minute Dancer,
  Barry Wallenstein
Water Music,
  Robert Haight
Dream of The Black Wolf,
  Keith Taylor

1994
Images Cadiennes (Cajun Images),
  Beverly Matherne
Palimpsest,
  Anne Hutchinson
Victrola,
  Danny Rendleman
Pierced By Sound,
  Lawrence Pike (Second Printing)
No Sporting Chance,
  K.C. Washington
The Hollow Moon,
  Edited by M. L. Liebler
The Red Eye Incident,
A Special Community Writing Project
A Service On The Sufficiency of Feeding Finches,
  Ben Bohnhorst
Bloodline Poems,
  Del Corey

1995
Convalescence and Other Poems,
  Tyrone Williams (Third Printing)
Great Lake,
  John R. Reed
Descent From The Cross,
  Ben Bohnhorst
Memory Bags,
  Thom Jurek
Zodiac Arrest,
  Rochelle Ratner
The Middle West,
  Danny Rendleman
Time Is Not Linear,
  Cindi St. Germain
Perfume And Tears,
  Ben Bohnhorst

1996
Peacocks & Beans,
  Valerie Tekavec
Letters to Che,
  Melba Joyce Boyd
I Want My Body Back,
  Ron Allen
Fweivel: The Day Will Come,
  Frazier Russell
Abstract Cores,
  Kim Webb
Living in the Fire Nest,
  Linda Nemec Foster
Mothering & Dream of Rain,
  Judith Kerman

1997
Too Soon To Leave,
  Steven Schreiner
Through the Straits, At Large,
  Anca Vlasopolos
Pardon My Allusions,
  Del Corey
Labor Day at Walden Pond,
  Edward Morin
Sudden Parade,
  Michael Lauchlan
Mountains to Motown,
  Edited by James M. Burdine
Bye Bye DDR,
  Eugene Chadbourne
Birdie On The Back Nine,
  William Boyer

1998
Working It Out,
  Larry Smith